Trickster in Texas

A Doctor Danger Mystery

HEATHER SILVIO

Panther Books

Panther Books: Tampa, FL & Portland, OR.

Visit the author's website at https://www.heathersilvio.com
Contact the author at: heather@heathersilvio.com

Cover design by Sonia Freitas at Chloe Belle Arts
https://www.ChloeBelleArts.com

Library of Congress Control Number: 2025904162
ISBN (Print) 9781951192419
ISBN (E-book) 9781951192402

BOOKS BY HEATHER SILVIO

DOCTOR DANGER MYSTERIES

Hazard in Hawaii (#1)

Spirits in Savannah (#2)

PARANORMAL TALENT AGENCY

Lights, Camera, Action (Episode One)

Reset to One (Episode Two)

That's a Wrap (Episode Three)

An Unexpected Sequel (Episode Four)

Jumping the Shark (Episode Five)

The Season Finale (Episode Six)

Paranormal Talent Agency Episode Collections

NON-SERIES FICTION

Not Quite Famous

Beyond the Abyss

Courting Death

NONFICTION

Special Snowflake Syndrome

Happiness by the Numbers

Stress Disorders: A Healing Path for PTSD

CHAPTER ONE

Fear swept over me, demolishing my internal protective wall. Before that moment, I would've said that the worst that could happen at an awards banquet was boring speeches. I gripped the arms of my chair, surveying the room while I tried to remain otherwise still.

I need to stay hidden. I can't be found out. Not until I finish my plan.

"Doc, are you alright?" Daniel Trawl, sitting next to me at the round table, whispered his question.

When my gaze found my assistant's, the concern in his hazel eyes grounded me, helping me realize that the thoughts and emotions I experienced weren't my own.

"Sarah? How can I help?"

I took several deep breaths, concentrating on the lingering peppery scent of the *cacio e pepe* main course, and willing my racing heart to slow. My internal protective wall was in a shambles and I needed to calm down to build it back. As a clairempath, my wall was the only thing keeping the physical and emotional experiences of others—human and, especially, supernatural—from subsuming me. I closed my eyes to focus inward on each crumbled stone block, first reassembling the bricks and then floating them upward to recreate the wall. When I no longer heard my heartbeat thundering in my ears, I paused. Choosing to leave a tiny hole in the protective wall, I opened my eyes and turned to Dan.

"Doc? What happened?" he asked.

Instead of answering, I stood. My inherent clumsiness chose that moment to surface. I wobbled on my sensible heels and my leg rocked the table, sloshing merlot in glasses just refilled by the circulating waitstaff.

"Is everything okay, Sarah?" My former boss, Jeffrey McCarthy, asked the question from his seat opposite me at the round six-top table. The ex-private investigator was also an ex-athlete, and his tall, full frame—if soft with age—dwarfed his petite wife, Chrissie, sitting beside him.

I gave a quick shake of my head, offering an uncertain smile. "I need to borrow Dan for a second. Make sure they leave me a dessert if someone comes by."

The other couple at the table chuckled before returning to their conversation. But not Jeff nor his wife. Jeff moved to stand, but Chrissie placed her hand on his tuxedo-clad arm and leaned over to whisper in his ear. Probably telling him to let me handle it. I smothered a smile; it was second nature for him to want to help. After all, he retired from the business I now ran. But if there was an issue, they knew I could manage it.

And there was definitely an issue. I turned from the table, traversing the other six-tops scattered throughout the ballroom. We were in a swanky hotel in Dallas, Texas, for the annual meeting of the National Association of Detectives. Even better, tonight's black-tie event was an awards banquet. Among the accolades, the association honored Jeff with a Lifetime Achievement Award. Given the heart troubles that resulted in a retirement he hadn't wanted, this was a crowning accomplishment in his illustrious career.

I scanned the crowd of well-dressed guests while I moved toward the spike of fear that pulsed against the tiny hole I'd left in my protective wall. Someone in this room was experiencing an off-the-charts level of fear, worry, and anxiety.

Unless there was a supernatural boost.

Something I was uniquely qualified to identify as a Supernatural Specialist. When I took over Jeff's investigative service—and Dan's *A Doctor Danger Mystery* blog blew up—it made perfect sense to offer niche services combining my supernatural abilities and expertise in comparative mythology. So far, business had been booming for my Tampa-based consulting firm.

I resumed scanning the room for the elevated emotions, while probing for a supernatural element. The emotional and physical drone of the crowd undulated in my mind like the waves created in a theme-park pool.

There.

On the far end of the room, just inside the main entrance to the banquet hall. I found the source of the emotion I was feeling. The woman wore a flowing red dress that, while lovely, was understated for black tie. I doubted she was an invited guest. Her head darted around, frantically scanning the room much as I had earlier.

Her brown eyes met my green ones. A cautious smile flitted across her face. She moved toward me and Dan as we redirected our movement toward her, each assessing the other upon approach. Taller than me, even in my heels. Long, curly hair like mine, but dark brown, where mine was auburn.

"Doctor Danger? Doctor Sarah Danger?" she asked with a slight Mexican accent.

"Yes," I answered, fear building again within me. *We're running out of time.* But for what?

The woman grabbed the sides of my arms.

"Hey!" Dan exclaimed and reached to remove her hands.

She leaned to whisper in my ear. "I need your help before someone else vanishes."

CHAPTER TWO

The woman released me. "I'm sorry," she said. "When I heard you were in town at the banquet, I had to find you."

"Heard I was in town?" I questioned.

She nodded at Dan. "I read in his blog that you both would be here tonight."

That explained it. Since Dan first published one of our supernatural cases in his blog, it had become a fabulous referral source, even if not everyone believed it was legitimate. I glanced around the perimeter of the room. "Come with me… um?"

"Isabel Garcia," she answered my unarticulated question. "Please, call me Isabel."

"Isabel. Come with me," I said over my shoulder, already moving. Isabel and Dan followed me to the edge of the room and then along the wall to the exit.

The ballroom spilled out into a foyer that was many decibels quieter than the banquet hall. I considered the area and sighted a small alcove on the far end with a couch and two chairs. Dan and Isabel followed me again as I led them to the seating area. Dan took the blue wingback chair, while Isabel and I perched on the matching couch. I rested my hands beside my crossed legs, one thumb absently brushing against the soft fabric of the couch.

Once seated, Isabel seemed at a loss for words. I'd sealed my wall of protection up tight to keep her from overwhelming me again, still uncertain if the emotion was so high naturally… or supernaturally. But her body language alone told me of her distress. She sat ramrod straight, hands gripping her thighs through her dress. Wide eyes stared unblinking at us. Lips thinned into an almost invisible line.

"Why were you looking for us?" I prompted her.

That was all it took. Isabel explained that two university students were missing, and a third was almost a victim. The first student vanished from downtown Wichita Falls, a small town also notable for an Air Force base. That had generated some interest since college students in small towns don't often just vanish. There was an additional undercurrent of thinking that perhaps she fled for personal reasons. Then a second student disappeared three days later. That stirred up more explicit concern, but the local police had nothing more to go on than in the first case. And then a third college student came forward three days after that with a wild story about how a bird tried to kidnap her while walking home from a bar.

"A bird?" Dan interjected his question with a chuckle.

"Yes," Isabel answered seriously. "A bird."

"What was the reaction to her story?" I asked, though I suspected the answer.

"Dismissed as being drunk. Nobody believed her." Sadness tinged her voice.

"You believe her," I stated this as a fact, not a question. Isabel nodded.

"Why? It sounds unlikely to be true," I pressed.

Her brown eyes squeezed shut. She opened them in time with a noisy exhale. Anxiety thumped against my internal barrier. My heart rate spiked in response until I brought it down by focusing on her as the source.

"Isabel, we can't help you if you don't tell us everything you know," I encouraged her in a hushed tone.

"I believe the disappearances are supernatural," she spit the words out rapid-fire.

"That's why you wanted to find Doctor Danger," Dan concluded, and Isabel nodded.

"Why do you believe the disappearances are supernatural? You believe a bird tried to abduct this college student, as well as the missing students?" I asked without inflection in order not to sway her story. If she thought I didn't believe her, she might not be as forthcoming.

"Have you heard of Lechuza?" Isabel asked in response.

At the word *Lechuza*, anxiety wrapped around me, pushing in on my chest and roiling my stomach. I coughed to relieve the pressure. The very idea of Lechuza caused Isabel so much distress that she pulsed with it.

Dan and I exchanged a glance. He couldn't feel the overwhelming emotions flowing around us, so all he had to react to was the word. His eyebrows knitting in confusion suggested unfamiliarity, but the name rang a bell for me.

"She's a witch who sometimes appears as a bird," I replied.

Isabel nodded. "There's more to it than that, of course, but yes. The rumor is that the bird who attempted to abduct the third college student is a Lechuza appearing in her owl form."

High levels of energy pinged all around me, trying to find a weak spot in my protection wall. The pings reminded me of the sharp shocks my physical body once experienced running through an obstacle course challenge consisting of dangling live wires that brushed against exposed skin. That convinced me Isabel was correct about there being a supernatural element to this case. Whether it was a Lechuza remained to be seen. As well as what role Isabel played, since the energy seemed to be following her or emanating from her. But either way, I'd made my decision.

"I'll take the case."

CHAPTER THREE

Thankfully, back at the banquet table, the others previously seated now stood socializing nearby, except for Jeff and Chrissie. Dan and I borrowed the empty seats and I explained what had happened in a whispered exchange with them.

"How certain are you that this isn't just a drunk girl's fantasy?" Jeff sipped his sparkling water.

I shrugged. "It is possible, of course," I allowed. "But I just don't think so. The woman who hired me—"

"Has she actually paid you anything?" Chrissie asked with a snort. I'd branded her a fire-cracker from the first time I'd met her; she always spoke her mind. Of course, it was also a reasonable question. She knew I was like her husband—a sucker for a sob story who wouldn't always request a deposit upfront.

Dan chuckled when I flushed. "Believe it or not," he said, "the client offered to complete our initial intake forms and transfer money for the retainer from her bank using her phone. She was that determined to have Sarah start right away."

Chrissie quirked an eyebrow. "That was handy."

"How did you leave it?" Jeff asked.

"I exchanged information with Isabel and assured her we would join her in Wichita Falls tomorrow to investigate."

"Which brings us back to my question," Jeff prompted.

I nodded. "Isabel had energy pouring off her at levels that almost certainly had to have a supernatural component. I'm confident there's something unusual happening in Wichita Falls. Whether the girl's story is just a drunk girl's story." I paused with another shrug. "That I won't know until I interview her."

. "It sounds like it should be an interesting case, regardless," Jeff said, his wistful tone catching me by surprise. He might not have chosen to leave the business, but I was under the impression he'd grown to like his life of leisure. There was one surefire way to check if he was enjoying retirement….

With a sly look at Chrissie, who stifled a giggle because she knew what I was about to do, I leaned toward Jeff. "Do you want to come with us to Wichita Falls?"

His brown eyes widened at the question and his ruddy complexion reddened further, but he stayed silent.

Chrissie turned to him. "Do you, honey?"

Jeff glanced at his wife and then at me before sighing. "As tempting as that is, you're perfectly capable of handling this on your own." He pointed at Dan. "Well, not entirely on your own, right?"

"I'll always follow the doc," Dan agreed with a wink at me. "Anywhere she wants to go."

I shook my head, this time at his mildly flirtatious tone and that wink. These types of exchanges had been part of our friendship from the beginning. Despite Dan being a very attractive man, I was his senior, both in age and now in employment. He'd started with Jeff as an intern like I had, but as he'd progressed toward his own doctorate in mythology, he'd also become my indispensable employee. Plus, I could never repay him for his blog putting my supernatural investigative services on the map. I would always care for him and be indebted to him, but he would remain a close friend and confidant.

"When I head up to my room," I said, pointedly ignoring Dan, "I'll message Mandie to start gathering info for us. She can research the first two victims, the third almost-victim, and the Lechuza that Isabel believes is behind everything."

CHAPTER FOUR

The drive from Dallas to Wichita Falls—home of Sheppard Air Force Base and Midwestern State University—was mostly highway driving past flat scrub brush and the occasional tree. Although, I was surprised to see the amount of construction, both roadwork and buildings. Maybe there'd been a population explosion in north Texas.

"I'm so glad to be out of that evening gown and into my jeans," I commented from the passenger seat to Dan, as I fiddled with the satellite radio. Normally I drove, but Dan had a discount code if we put the car under his name. So, I accepted my passive role to save the money.

"I looked like everybody else in my penguin suit, but you were stunning," he replied offhand. "The deep emerald complemented you."

"Flattery will get you nowhere, junior," I quipped, indeed feeling flattered, and recognizing the sweet intent behind the comment. Plus, he probably wasn't wrong about the emerald color of my flowing bias-cut gown accenting my green eyes and auburn hair. "Tuxedos are a good look for almost all men," I said, before redirecting away from a potentially awkward conversation. "Let me check in with Mandie."

"You know you want to pick that station," Dan said as a popular 80s song played. He knew that was my favorite decade of music.

I stopped pressing radio buttons and pulled my phone out of my backpack. A quick check of email and texts followed. "She said she's gathering info, but it's slow going, and to check in with her later."

"Okay, cool," he acknowledged the relayed update.

"I'll let the client know we'll be in town soon and unless she has something new, we'll want to start interviewing before meeting with her again."

"Sounds good, boss," Dan replied.

I called Isabel Garcia. Dan's head swung my way when I said *Kimberly Roberts*, our possible attempted-kidnapping victim.

"What's up?" he asked when I ended the call.

"Isabel said she reached out to Kimberly, and she agreed to meet us at a local coffeeshop."

"Excellent."

The *Welcome to Wichita Falls* sign came into view, informing us that the city had "*Blue Skies. Golden*

Opportunities" and was the home of Sheppard AFB. "We're almost there." Anticipation bubbled up at the potential of a new supernatural case. I typically managed several cases a month with my adjunct faculty schedule, and I loved stretching my clairempathic muscles to help people.

Dan and I headed straight for the coffeeshop to meet potential victim number three. We scored a parking spot right in front of the building on 8th Street and entered the cute establishment. Tons of natural light flooded in from the floor-to-ceiling windows covering two walls. I scanned the interior, looking for Kimberly Roberts. The heavenly scent of brewing coffee filled the cafe.

An early-twenties female sat on a brown, tufted bench settee against one of the windowed walls. She stared down at the paper coffee cup cradled in her hands. I released a stone from my internal barrier and filtered the energy that rushed through the opening to focus on the young woman in a vintage Led Zeppelin concert t-shirt and jeans. For a moment, worry about what would happen next surfaced, followed by sadness about being here at all. Her hyperawareness of the other patrons in the coffeeshop clinched it for me. A woman who'd nearly been kidnapped wouldn't want to have to relive it by recounting the event, and her worry about something else happening would result in needing to pay close attention to those around her. Without question, I'd identified our attempted kidnapping victim.

Replacing the stone in my protection wall, I stepped forward, Dan following my lead. We crossed the space, our shoes silent on the stylized brick floor. She glanced up when we reached her.

"Kimberly Roberts?" I asked. At her wordless nod, I continued. "I'm Doctor Sarah Danger, and this is my associate, Daniel Trawl. Thank you so much for agreeing to meet with us." I sat beside her, leaving a cushion of distance, while Dan took the chair next to the settee. In my peripheral vision, I saw him remove his tablet from the backpack at his feet.

"I wasn't sure when that woman—Isabel something?—first reached out on social media." Kimberly's brown eyes filled with tears. "But when she said you might be able to help me make sense of what happened…" she trailed off. Her sneaker-clad foot tapped on the floor.

"We'll do our best," I assured her. "I see your coffee cup is empty. Would you like another?" I offered, in part to help calm her.

Her foot stopped tapping as she considered my question. "No, thank you," she declined, before explaining, "I'm a bit sensitive to mood-altering substances." A rueful smile brightened her face. "I'll be bouncing off the walls if I have another one."

I matched her smile. "Understood." After a quick internal debate, I removed several stones from my barrier. One way to test if there was a supernatural element was to let her energy come at me. It was a calculated risk. "Tell me what happened on the night someone tried to kidnap you."

She ran her hands through her short blond hair while she gathered her thoughts.

Dan had his stylus at the ready to take notes on what she told us. I waited, curious about where she'd start the story. When she spoke, it quickly became a high-wire balancing act between hearing the events in her words and experiencing them in my mind as if it had happened to me.

"A group of us went to The Broken Tap after a really tough final," Kimberly began. "That's a local bar," she added. "It's fun, low-key. You can grab a drink and shoot some pool. You don't have to worry about anything happening." The sides of her mouth drooped. "Normally, anyway."

"Did anything happen outside the normal while you were at the bar?" I asked, accepting the spike of fear that blossomed out from her to encompass me.

"No!" she snapped, then inhaled and exhaled a shaky breath.

My stomach tightened with her inhalation and relaxed along with her exhale.

"That's what's so difficult. Nothing weird happened. And, yes, I had a drink. But, no, I wasn't drunk." Her voice took on a defiant tone, and I suspected the police had grilled her on this point.

How dare the police challenge me!

I quickly identified the thought as not driven by my own defiance. "Just one drink?" I asked, attempting to stabilize the emotional energy surging within me.

"Yes, just one. I don't respond well to alcohol either. I learned that when I turned 21 last year." She snorted. "Have you ever felt like you wanted to die? After only three drinks? Yeah, that was me. I've learned that if I stick with one regular drink, I'm fine."

"Who was with you that night?" I asked.

She listed four women's names and phone numbers, which Dan noted in our case file.

"Do you mind if I speak to these women?"

She grimaced.

I clarified, "To see if they noticed anything suspicious that you might have missed."

My words appeared to mollify her somewhat. "Sure. Whatever. I'd really like for people to quit acting like I hallucinated because of drinking too much."

I started to huff along with her about everyone being judgmental but caught myself. Again accepting and dismissing Kimberly's emotion, I refocused. "Did anyone talk to you at the bar?"

"I mean, we spoke to the bartender and the woman who came around collecting empties. Other than that, not that I recall." She shrugged.

"How long were you and your friends at the bar?"

"A few hours. I honestly didn't check my phone."

At my quirked eyebrow, she reddened.

"Okay, yes, I checked social media, of course." She rolled her eyes. "But I didn't make a note of the time."

"Fair enough."

"Becca still had a mid-morning final the next day, so I'm certain it couldn't have been much past midnight when we left."

"You left together?"

"We walked out together." She swallowed with an audible click. "The others rode together. They live nearer to each other. I live at the Holt, which is within walking distance of The Broken Tap."

"The Holt?"

"Apartment building. It's just a one-bedroom/one-bath place my parents help pay for," Kimberly answered.

"So your friends left by car, and you walked the few blocks back to your apartment building," I confirmed.

"It's not even a few blocks. It's literally around the corner." She frowned. "Well, it's around the corner and maybe a block and a half up. It's not far."

She sounded defensive, so I complimented her. "It sounds like you're very familiar with the area."

"Yes," she agreed, nodding like a bobblehead. "It's very safe. It never occurred to me…" she trailed off.

"None of this is your fault."

"Even though I was drinking," she snapped.

Clairempathic guilt spiked within me from Kimberly's shame over her perceived lapse in judgement. "No," I declared. My assurance calmed us both.

She sagged back against the settee. "I waved as they drove away," she continued her story in a low voice. "When I turned right, at the corner, onto 8th—" She pointed toward the street. "—a flash of something caught my eye in the parking lot on the other side of the street."

"Could you identify the flash?"

"It was odd. Almost like how in the movies someone flicks a flashlight off and on, like a signal?" she answered, her statement ending in a questioning inflection.

"You thought that was odd."

"I did. That's why I crossed the street."

"Any traffic?"

"No. It's not super busy during the week."

"What happened on the other side of the street?"

Her foot started tapping on the brick floor again.

I don't want to talk about this. Why do I have to keep talking about this?

The quick anxious thoughts had to be triggered by her anxiety. I struggled to keep them segregated from my own thoughts.

She broke eye contact.

I surrounded her pulsing emotions in an internal bubble and released them. "There's no judgment here," I reassured the young woman. "I'm just trying to help understand what happened and find the missing students."

Her foot stilled. She lifted her coffee cup to her lips before remembering it was empty. "That's when the bird tried to kidnap me," she stated flatly.

"Let's back up a minute. How soon after you crossed the street did you see the bird?"

Kimberly stared at the ground.

I waited her out. The uncertainty, fear, and incredulity within me rose dangerously high, forcing me to replace one of the stones I'd removed from my wall. I almost sighed in relief at the instantaneous muting of her ceaseless emotional waves.

"Not immediately," she answered. "I stepped off the road onto this grassy area and it wasn't until I looked up that I saw it."

"What did you see?"

Her eyes bored into mine. "A man-sized bird."

Nobody believes me. They all think I was drunk. Or crazy.

This time, I recognized even faster that these thoughts were a reaction to Kimberly's despair. I couldn't risk replacing another stone in my barrier. Did Kimberly hallucinate, see a person dressed in a bird costume, or was it truly a supernatural being, like a Lechuza? Now would be the time for a supernatural component to appear, if there was one.

"A man-sized bird," she repeated as if interpreting my silence as disbelief.

"Did you recognize what kind of bird it was?" I asked.

She tensed and shook her head. "It had white feathers," she offered with a one-shoulder shrug. "Maybe if I hadn't been so startled, I would have noticed more."

"That's okay. You're doing great." I placed my hand atop hers that still cradled the empty coffee cup. A shot of jealousy rocked my mind and my fingers tightened on Kimberly's.

Mine.

"Are you okay, Doctor Danger?" she asked, pulling away from my grasping fingers.

I scrutinized the interior of the coffeeshop. That emotion and thought hadn't come from Kimberly, and it certainly wasn't mine. But whose? My gaze flitted around the room, stopping to rest on faces where I could see them. Many people had their heads facing computer screens or buried in books. The emotion faded and I refocused on Kimberly. "Apologies. I was... distracted," I said, noting that Dan watched me with undisguised concern.

"That's okay," Kimberly said. My disruption of the conversational flow reduced her discomfort, so that was a silver lining.

"Did it look like a person in a bird costume?" I resumed my questioning.

She shook her head hard. "That's the really crazy thing, Doctor Danger. It didn't. It looked like a big, white-feathered bird."

"Could it have been an owl?" Asking leading questions was an investigative no-no, but Isabel believed it was a Lechuza, and she'd confirmed that a Lechuza's animal form was an owl.

"I... don't know," she stumbled. "I don't think so. I just remember it being big, with white feathers."

"What happened next?"

Tears filled her eyes. "It rushed at me. I remember screaming, which caused it to stop and... make noises."

An empathic feminine howl rose in my mind, followed by a series of rapid clucking. I blinked a few times to refocus my attention. I believed the howl came from Kimberly, not the unidentified earlier source. The howl lacked the primal urgency of that previous energy. "I know you screamed, but did you clearly hear the noises?"

"Yes. Sort of a, I don't know, clucking sound." She demonstrated, and it sounded eerily like what my clairempathy had manifested, a series of short, staccato notes. To my knowledge, owls didn't cluck, so I wasn't sure what this meant for Isabel's theory.

At the sound of the clucking, a tsunami of anger and anxiety swamped my mind.

What is she doing! How does she remember that?

I gasped and with tremendous effort tried again to identify the source of the thoughts and emotions. The use of the pronoun *she* confirmed for me that these weren't Kimberly's experiences. Whoever they belonged to had higher supernatural energy than even had surrounded Isabel.

"Doc?" This time Dan asked the question, distracting me from my hunt for the source of the energy. Both Dan and Kimberly stared at me.

I shook my head, trying to dislodge the cloying experiences. "Apologies, again. Something in here is triggering me," I said, mostly to Dan, though Kimberly nodded. I needed to get back on track, while remaining attentive to the others in the coffeeshop. "How far away would you guess the bird was at that point?" I asked, trying to determine if the bird should have been close enough for Kimberly to see details.

"Um, I'm not sure. I was standing on the edge of the grassy area that's between the street and the lot. It could have been ten or fifteen feet still."

I did quick calculations in my head. "When you first saw the bird, it would have been further back in the parking lot?" And further in the dark, I added silently. Maybe it was a person in a costume after all.

"I think so?" she answered, uncertain.

"What happened next?" I asked.

"I didn't even think. Before it started moving toward me again, I bolted down the block to my building entrance."

"Did the bird follow you?"

She gave another wide-eyed shrug. "I have no idea," she admitted. "I didn't look back. I don't even think I took a breath until I was back in my apartment with the door locked behind me."

"I assume you told all of this to the police?"

Her expression darkened. "I did. There are no cameras on any of the buildings in that area, so they dismissed me as another drunk college student."

"But they at least believe something happened?" I asked, the shared emotions subsiding after I replaced the final stone in my protection wall. I'd learned everything I was going to about the supernatural element from this conversation.

A single tear tracked down her face. "I'm not sure they would, but since two others disappeared first…"

"Did you know either of those women?"

A wordless shake of her head and another lone tear fell. "I could have been next," she whispered.

"But you weren't," I reminded her.

"No, I wasn't," she agreed, her voice stronger. "Will you let me know what you find out?" she asked.

"Of course."

We said our goodbyes, and then Kimberly stood to leave. I stood with her, watching in my peripheral vision to see if anyone else moved. As Kimberly made her way to the door, several other patrons did as well.

My clairempathy wasn't pulling anything more from the odd source from earlier.

Could it have been Kimberly, after all?

I didn't think so.

"Give me a sec," I said to Dan, then turned toward the door myself. A stream of people moved in and out through the doorway.

A man paused within its frame and turned back. Our eyes met. Pulsating waves of frustration and anger knocked me back despite my fully composed internal barrier. I stumbled over my feet and crashed back onto the couch, hurriedly making mental notes about the man. Average height. Slim build. Curly brown hair. Bright blue, magnetic eyes.

Before I could rise from the couch to follow, he disappeared through the door and into the crowd on the street.

CHAPTER FIVE

"Doc, what happened? Are you okay?" Dan asked, his hand gripping my elbow. He lowered his voice. "Did you get supernatural energy from Kimberly?"

"No," I answered the last question. "There was someone else." I shook my head, attempting to clear the cobwebs that clogged my memory.

Dan peered around the room, but of course, there was nobody. "Who?"

"He was…" I trailed off, unable to retrieve the details. A hazy outline of a male in the doorway grew hazier the more I tried to grab it. "It's gone."

"What's gone?"

"The memory of who triggered my reaction." The hairs on the back of my neck stood up like they were going to war. This couldn't be good.

"What happened?" Dan's voice seemed to tighten with concern.

"I don't know," I answered honestly before getting back down to business. "Whatever it was will reveal itself in due course, I'm sure. In the meantime, we continue our investigative plan."

"What do you think about Kimberly's account of what happened?" he asked, rolling with my need to resume normal operations.

"I think we need to find out what Mandie learned about Lechuza. And we need to speak to Kimberly's friends who were with her that night."

While Dan stood in line to get us a couple of lattes, and knowing people's penchants to not answer calls from unknown numbers, I texted Kimberly's girlfriends who were with her that night. I encouraged them to confirm with Kimberly that I was legit. I assumed they did so, as they agreed to meet me at the coffeeshop. Dan had already returned with my mocha latte and was reviewing his notes while I responded to the final text.

"Drunk girl in denial, or something supernatural?" Dan asked. His hunter-green button-down polo shirt brought out the kaleidoscope of color in his hazel eyes, visible behind frameless glasses.

"Neither," I answered.

"That seems unlikely," he hedged, "given what happened when she left."

I laughed. "From Kimberly's perspective, it's neither. I believe her when she says she wasn't drunk."

"She did say she has a sensitivity to substances," he agreed. "Why not supernatural?"

"Although the intensity of her experience crashed repeatedly against my protective wall, there was nothing that felt like supernatural energy from her. Of course," I continued my train of thought with a slight frown, "that's not an absolute indication of anything."

"It's not?" he asked, although I recognized he was just helping to prompt my thought process. We'd worked together long enough that we knew best how to motivate and spur the other.

"No," I answered anyway. "Especially given what happened afterward. But, even that could have any number of mundane explanations. The man I'd sensed could have simply been a patron angry at the world because he'd lost a job, his wife left him, or any of a thousand other painful, but non-supernatural life events." A sliver of worry wormed its way into my mind, but was soon gone, along with the inciting incident, as if neither had happened at all. "As for Kimberly, it's been days since she encountered the attempted kidnapper. If that individual was of a supernatural bent, anything residual likely would have dissipated by now."

"What's next then?"

I checked the time on my phone. "It's still either a person in a bird suit or somehow a man-sized bird. Maybe a Lechuza, if Isabel is correct. Even though Kimberly said it clucked and she didn't recall it looking like an owl. Let's check in with Mandie and see what she's learned. We have time before Kimberly's friend, Becca, gets here."

Dan sat beside me, his leg nearly touching my own. He opened his tablet and we started a video chat with Amanda Jenkins, the researcher on my team. We'd met in graduate school, though her degree was in library science. She had a harried family life, but wouldn't ever trade her happy marriage and four children for the jet-setting life that Dan and I sometimes had.

"Hey guys," Mandie greeted us the moment her smiling face came onto the screen. She wore her brown curly hair in a loose ponytail that allowed many strands of hair to escape the band, and her hazel eyes—more brown than Dan's—sparkled at seeing us. "How's it going?"

I summarized our interview with Kimberly Roberts, the attempted kidnapping victim, including that she couldn't identify the bird, but that it was white and rapid-fire clucked at her.

Mandie startled me by smiling at this news. "That's not inconsistent with what I learned."

"It's not?" Dan asked.

She shook her head. "You're right, Doc, that a Lechuza usually appears as an owl. Of course, you know owls can be white, but you might be surprised to learn that sometimes they cluck."

"Huh. Who knew owls could cluck?"

"On the other hand, since the victim doesn't recall the bird resembling an owl, that doesn't support the Lechuza theory. On the other, other hand, we know that the victim's memory might not be reliable. Regardless, there's a much more important piece of information. A Lechuza often appears before someone is going to die," Mandie continued.

"Wait, what?" Dan asked, aghast. "Does that mean the other two kidnap victims are dead?"

"We're getting ahead of ourselves," I said, placing my hand on Dan's knee. "Mandie, why don't you start at the beginning?"

"Are you ready for a crash course in the mythology of Lechuza?" she responded. At our nods, her eyes strayed offscreen, most likely to review her notes on a second monitor. Some of the information I figured I would remember from my comparative mythology studies, but I knew that I definitely lost details.

"There are various Lechuza legends," Mandie began, "but they all originated from Hispanic folklore, and they all involved women."

"There are never male Lechuza?" Dan asked.

"Not that I found," Mandie answered. "In some legends, she sold her soul to the devil for magical powers. In others, she was a murdered woman's transformed spirit."

"Those are very different origin stories," I commented. "Interesting that in one legend, she's opportunistic and in the other, she's the victim."

"That dichotomy continues with her actions, too," Mandie said. "Depending on the legend, she might hunt people—anyone from babies to adults—or she might warn people that someone close to them will die."

"I'd be curious if the soul-selling version aligns with the hunting-people actions, and the murdered-woman version aligns with the warning-people of impending doom actions," I mused aloud.

Mandie tilted her head. "There was no clear-cut alignment that I saw, but that would be interesting, if the legends started that way."

"It seems logical, given possible intent," Dan said. "Although, I suppose we should be careful not to judge. These are just legends and there could be other mechanisms for a Lechuza to manifest."

"One hundred percent," I agreed.

"In terms of appearance, lechuza is Spanish for owl, so in most of the legends, a Lechuza appeared as either a white owl or a harpy with an owl body and a woman's face. She could be anywhere from four feet to seven feet tall and even have a 15-foot wingspan."

I considered the beauty of that. A seven-foot-tall owl-woman with a 15-foot wingspan. How incredible to see!

"Anything in the literature about how likely it is for a Lechuza to be a giant white owl with no human features, versus the owl-woman combo?" I asked.

Mandie shook her head. "Most sources said she usually appears as an owl with a woman's face."

"That's not what Kimberly remembers seeing," I said, drumming my fingers on my thigh. "That doesn't seem to be a tick in the Lechuza category."

"Kimberly could be misremembering," Dan said. "She did say all she remembered was a bird with white feathers. Maybe it is the less common appearance?"

"Absolutely," I agreed. "Anything else?"

"To be honest, most of what I read suggested that a Lechuza is one of two things. Either a folktale boogeyman intended to keep kids in line by parents threatening that she'll come for them if they misbehave. Or she's more of a reactive being that appears to provide a warning of some kind. I can't find anything in the literature about Lechuza kidnapping people."

We sat in silence, processing where this knowledge fit with what we'd learned.

In my peripheral vision, I watched a young woman approach where Dan and I sat.

"Doctor Danger?" she whispered.

"Yes," I said and gave the young lady my full attention, while Dan relocated to his seat on the wingback chair and made our silent goodbyes to Mandie. The woman was tall enough to be an athlete of some kind, with short black hair and piercing green eyes, even brighter than mine. Her hands rested on the skin visible between her body-hugging blue leggings and white crop top.

"I'm Becca Ross," she said, her soft voice somehow even quieter than her whisper. "I was with Kim the night of the... incident."

Though I stood to greet her, I did not offer my hand. Becca felt closed off and scared; I didn't want to spook her further. At my gesture to the seat Dan had occupied earlier, she sat quickly, wrapping her arms around her bare midriff.

"Hi Becca, it's nice to meet you." I eased into the interview and she gradually relaxed. Unfortunately, she neither saw nor heard anything useful, either at the bar or after their group left. Later, the other women who'd been at the bar that night with Kimberly repeated the same story.

By the time the coffeeshop closed at 2 pm, Dan and I had learned nothing new. On the plus side, the women confirmed that Kimberly rarely drank, and they all recalled that she only had one drink that night. But, unfortunately, they left in their car, just as Kimberly had said, and did not witness what she reported after.

Despite the lack of learning new information from Kimberly's girlfriends, I pondered the afternoon. My brain kept suggesting I missed something, but I couldn't fathom the cause. Our interviews yielded straightforward information, albeit not super-helpful. When Dan and I strode toward the coffeeshop door to leave, the strangest sense of déjà vu rocked me. What did that mean, if anything?

And, more importantly, given the interviews' lack of information leading to next steps… now what?

CHAPTER SIX

An unexpected call offered an early check-in, so Dan drove us to the chain hotel where we'd gotten two rooms. My uncertainty grew as I reviewed our notes during the drive. Isabel had seemed so certain it was a Lechuza responsible for the disappearances—and she had plenty of supernatural energy flowing around her—but something seemed off.

At the check-in desk, the man in the starched suit behind the counter startled when I said my name. "Is there an issue?" I asked.

"No, ma'am." His eyes darted over my shoulder.

I turned to see a man striding toward us, his eyes zeroed in on mine with a heightened intensity.

"What is this?" I asked the check-in attendant, my eyes never leaving the man in the blue sport coat over dark jeans and cowboy boots. "Is this the reason we got an early check-in?" The man in the sport coat saved the clerk from a stammered reply.

"Doctor Danger? Doctor Sarah Danger?" the man asked me. He had to be about my age, though of course much taller, with sharp blue eyes and buzz-cut blond hair. A light cedarwood scent tickled my nose.

I quirked an eyebrow. "Yes. And you are?"

He held out a card. *Detective Brad Snyder, Wichita Falls Police Department.*

"How did you know I was staying here, Detective?" I asked, trying and failing not to keep an incredulous tone.

He grinned. "It's a small town, ma'am. When I was told of your arrival, it only took a few calls to narrow down where you were staying."

"That hardly seems legal without a warrant." In all honesty, I knew it was legal. It just rankled a bit that he got here before we even did.

His smile dropped. "The law states that they can confirm whether you are a guest of the hotel, but not the exact room unless you have explicitly instructed them not to do so."

A quick relaxing of my protective wall allowed a normal amount of curiosity and concern to flow from the detective. He wasn't supernatural and he was here for a reason that likely overlapped with mine. "Relax, Detective Snyder," I replied with a crooked smile. Dan stifled a chuckle beside me. "What can I do for you?"

"Do you have a few minutes to talk?" he asked, pointing toward a corner of the hotel lobby.

"Of course," I agreed, and followed him, our footsteps silent on the rug over the hardwood floors to the far side of the lobby, well outside of the desk clerk's earshot.

He stopped beside a low, round, wood-look table surrounded by four circular, blue, ottoman chairs of matching height. The three of us sat on the chairs.

"Who told you of my arrival?" I asked out of curiosity. He was right. This was a small town. Maybe I could use that familiarity to my advantage.

"An off-duty deputy overheard you at the coffeeshop."

"That makes sense. How did you find this hotel specifically? I mean, the town's not *that* small."

He laughed. "That one took a bit more. I decided that a doctor wouldn't want a vacation rental aimed at the college student market, so I started with the highest-rated bigger-name hotels. It didn't take too many calls."

"Very good, Detective," I said, impressed despite myself. Maybe we could work together on this.

"Thank you very much, Doc," he said.

We shared amiable smiles. He used the nickname my team gave me before I'd even earned my doctorate. It had been a running joke for most of my all-but-dissertation time in graduate school.

"That being said, the Wichita Falls Police Department has this handled, ma'am. With respect, we don't need your help."

Guess we wouldn't be working together. "You don't?" I questioned, ignoring Dan's outright snort of laughter.

"Let the professionals do our jobs," he continued as if I hadn't spoken and Dan hadn't laughed.

"Well," I replied, drawing out the syllable a touch. "I am a professional, Detective, and my client believes my team can be of service."

"Your client?"

"You know I'm not going to disclose that."

"I've read your blog and your unusual cases are, shall we say, unique. Your team is professional," he allowed. "I could be difficult and remind you that you aren't a licensed professional in my jurisdiction."

"You could," I agreed. "Except don't we want the same thing?"

"And that is?"

"To get the missing women back and apprehend the kidnapper."

"If there is one," he added, but it seemed so rote, even I didn't believe he believed it.

"You don't believe the women ran away, do you?" I asked.

He eyed me and Dan for a moment and then sighed. "No, I do not. Especially not after someone grabbed for the third woman."

"Grabbed?" I exchanged a surprised look with Dan. Kimberly hadn't mentioned that the "birdman" had physically touched her.

"Keep this on deep background?"

"I'm not a reporter, but sure, I won't tell anyone what you tell me," I assured him, noting with pleasure that Dan had removed his tablet from his backpack to take notes.

"That's part of why everyone believed the third victim was drunk. Her story hasn't been consistent," he acknowledged.

"Interesting," I said as a placeholder while I searched my memories from our interview with Kimberly Roberts. Nothing. There was no indication that she was confused, or uncertain, other than what type of bird tried to kidnap her. She absolutely did not say that the bird ever laid hands—or would it be wings?—on her.

"What did she tell you?" he asked.

"In the interests of cooperation," I began with a half-smile, then recounted our interview with Kimberly.

"Interesting," the detective echoed my placeholder word. "That's close, but not quite what she told me, which was close, but not quite what she told the other two LEOs who interviewed her."

"Where are the discrepancies?" I asked. "Perhaps that will help us narrow down why the story is changing. Everyone's memory changes with retellings, but for this to happen so quickly, and in such major ways, seems suspect."

"The first big discrepancy was telling me, but nobody else, that the individual she described as a bird touched her arm, trying to drag her toward the back of the parking lot."

"How did she describe that? What the touch felt like, what she thought was happening?"

He considered my questions. "She struggled with that, kept insisting it just felt like rough feathers. But strong. Stronger than anyone pulled her before."

"She told me it couldn't have been a man in a bird costume. If the attacker was that strong, what's the likelihood it was a woman?"

"Seems unlikely," he agreed.

"So, we're truly thinking bird, or birdman?"

"She also said she felt unsteady, and that the man, or birdman," he used my word with a slight smirk, "was trying to bring her somewhere."

"Unsteady?"

"Exactly. She kept insisting she only had one drink. But when she described feeling unsteady…"

"Hmm, okay. There are clear inconsistencies. Interestingly, they seem centered on knowledge that might help in identifying the birdman," I concluded.

"That's a good catch, Doc," he said.

"Try not to sound surprised."

Detective Snyder reached inside his coat to remove a small notepad from a pocket. He flipped it open to reveal a folded sheet of paper. "It's a photocopy," he explained, "of a sketch artist's drawing of what Kimberly Roberts told us she saw."

I set the paper on the table before us and took my phone out of my backpack. "May I?"

"Don't share it with anyone," he reminded me.

"Anyone but my client," I conditionally agreed. I angled the image this way and that, examining the artist's drawing of the bird that attacked Kimberly before taking several photographs of the beautifully rendered sketch. And if accurate, absolutely terrifying. "If this came after me, my mind might forget what had happened too," I speculated.

"That's a definite possibility," Detective Snyder agreed.

Of course, I let go unsaid the possibility that a supernatural being caused someone to forget what they'd seen.

Dan and I stared at the sketch.

"It's clearly a bird," he said.

"And clearly a turkey," I added. "Why would Kimberly not be able to remember that it looked like a turkey?"

"Maybe because it's a white turkey, which I don't think is something that occurs in nature," the detective answered. "Is this why your client hired you? Is there a supernatural component to my case?"

I appreciated his directness, so I responded the same. "Yes, my client believes there is a supernatural component to your case."

"Can you share with me what that might be?"

I thought about it, then shook my head. "Without knowing how all of this ties in with my client, I can't."

He cocked his head as he assessed me, perhaps deciding whether to push for the information. "Understood," he finally said. "Will you at least consider sharing actionable intel with us?"

"Yes," I agreed. "That I can do." I withdrew a business card from my backpack and handed it to him, adding, "Since our goals are the same."

"I'll reciprocate when I can," the detective responded as he accepted the card. He stood from his chair. Dan and I rose to match.

"We appreciate that," I said.

"Stay safe, Doc," he said, offering a firm handshake.

"You too," I responded.

Dan waited until the automatic doors to the outside world had closed behind the detective before he spoke. "A turkey is not an owl."

"No, it is not."

"What do you think?" he asked.

"I think that tons of supernatural energy poured off of Isabel Garcia when we met her in Dallas. It's time we had another chat with Ms. Garcia."

CHAPTER SEVEN

The time it took me to recognize that Isabel Garcia overflowed with supernatural energy left me scrambling to return the stones I'd removed from my internal wall of protection. She was either the source of the energy or she was often around the source. I would tread carefully during this follow-up interview until I could discern which.

Dan, Isabel, and I sat on the same ottoman chairs around the same table we'd sat around with the detective. It seemed easier than trying to meet somewhere else. Other than the folks checking in across the lobby, we still had the space to ourselves. Nevertheless, we kept our voices pitched low.

"What have you learned?" Isabel asked, her weak, shaky voice suggesting anxiety.

Even though we had unspecified concerns about Isabel, she was still the client, so I brought her up to speed on everything we'd learned. The energy spiking from her during the recounting of Kimberly Roberts' near-abduction almost knocked me off my chair. I held back, though, doling out the detective's information like breadcrumbs. Isabel expressed surprise that law enforcement was willing to work with us.

"The benefits of hiring a professional as a liaison," I reminded her.

She offered a tired smile in response. "Thank you for the summary," she added.

"There's one more thing," I said, set to observe her reaction. We'd reached the moment I'd been waiting for. I visualized my internal stone barrier rising from the floor of my mind to infinity. Taking a calculated risk, I then removed just a pebble from near the bottom, hoping to mitigate the expected onslaught. Energy swarmed at the opening, attempting to push through. I concentrated on the feelings of overwhelm and fear erupting within me. The foreignness of the isolated emotions flared in my mind and I recognized the feelings were from Isabel.

What if they find out?

Find out what, Isabel? I wondered as I tightened down my thoughts. My skin crawled, like it surged with static electricity. Could there be that much free-floating energy in the room? I'd interacted with a possible goddess in the past, and even that energy felt less than what I sensed now.

"Are you okay?" Dan said at the same time Isabel asked, "You said there was one more thing?"

I gasped at the tightness in my body, the tension begging me to flee, but warring with the worry that more women would vanish if I did. The energy needed to be released. I pinpointed the isolated supernatural energy in my mind. Using my bubble technique, I encircled as much of that energy as I could and imagined the bubbles rising from my mind into the atmosphere. Everything dropped enough for me to function.

I fumbled with my cellphone on the table. "As I said, during our interview with Kimberly she said she wasn't sure what kind of bird she saw, just that it was man-sized and had white feathers." I opened the photo I'd taken of the sketch artist's drawing and turned the phone to Isabel.

An unreadable emotion flashed across her face before she clamped it down.

But the supernatural energy. It roared in response. I grabbed my head with my hands and leaned over between my legs.

I heard Dan and Isabel calling my name through the morass of emotions.

We won't save the women. Nothing can be done. There will be more.

Tears streamed down my face while I strove to identify the source of distress as Isabel's emotions and thoughts. I didn't understand the physical pain I was experiencing or the sentences fluttering through my mind. I'd evaluate those after I replaced my stone.

No. Replaced my *pebble.* This reaction was from removing a solitary pebble from my protection wall.

With concerted effort, I visualized lifting and replacing that single pebble back into my protective wall. The pulse of Isabel's supernatural energy pushed back, challenging my ability to replace the small stone. I grunted with the effort, before my mind succeeded in shoving the pebble into the wall's gap. The forcefulness required left me panting and unable to focus on anything but recovering.

I held my breath for several seconds, then blew it out in a rush. Sitting back up, I used my fingers to wipe the tears from my cheeks.

A hand touched my elbow.

"Doc? Sarah?"

I met Dan's concerned gaze and offered a wobbly grin. "Give me a second. I'll be okay." For a few moments, I concentrated on Dan's hand, grounding me in the physical world, and kicked out all of Isabel's remaining supernatural energy.

Isabel.

I switched my focus to her, and while her expression showed concern, she telegraphed guilt, too. I considered asking her who—no, what—she was, then reconsidered. She had a lot of fear. It was unlikely the women were at risk because of her. Regardless, she knew more than she had told us.

"You recognize the image." I pointed at my phone, which she still held.

She dropped it on the wooden table. It clattered in our silence.

"What is it? What is its significance to this case?"

"I don't know," she replied, though it was unclear whether that was the answer to the first question, second question, or both. I'd made a cardinal interviewing mistake of asking more than one question at a time.

"You hired us," I reminded her, changing my approach, gentling my voice, like talking to a skittish animal. "We can't do our jobs effectively if you withhold information."

She shook her head. "I don't know its significance to this case," she insisted. "Why did you react that way?" she asked, not answering my other question.

"You read Dan's blog, right?"

Understanding dawned on her face. "That's what the clairempathy is like?"

"Yes," I answered, weariness settling in my bones.

"That looked rough," she admitted.

"It can be when I'm around high amounts of supernatural energy."

She flushed but maintained her stance. "I wish I could be more help. I want the answers as much as you do. Probably more so. At least it seems you've eliminated the possibility of it being a Lechuza."

Her jump to concluding there had been no Lechuza involvement surprised me. "Did we?" I asked.

"A Lechuza appears as an owl. We might not know the turkey's significance," she continued, "but it's not an owl."

"Yes, that's true," I agreed, feeling I was missing something, but unsure what it was.

Isabel jerked up from her seat. Dan and I were slower to follow suit.

"Thank you for the information," she said, her tone cordial but distant. "I appreciate it. Please continue to update me. If I learn anything, I'll let you know."

Before I could open my mouth to respond to her formality, she spun and flew across the room. A moment before she disappeared from the lobby, she brought a cellphone to her ear.

Who—or what—was so important that she was calling mere seconds after leaving our meeting?

CHAPTER EIGHT

The next morning found Dan and me in a corner of the hotel dining area, eating the complimentary breakfast, while researching Isabel Garcia. We felt a little foolish for not having done so when I first had my strong supernatural reaction to her presence. But, in our defense, it never occurred to us that she'd be involved in the disappearances, given that she hired us.

"I didn't realize how hungry I was," I said as I took another bite of my everything bagel smothered in cream cheese.

Dan chuckled but said nothing as he forked some egg into his mouth.

I wiped the corners of my mouth with a napkin and sighed. "Hopefully you and Mandie are doing better than

I am. From what I'm seeing, our Isabel Garcia has zero identifiable social media presence."

"I'm not having better luck, unfortunately. I've used our usual company for searching and her name is too common for them to find anything. Without a birthdate, birth city, or even just a middle name to narrow things down, there's just too much out there." He sipped from his coffee, eyes narrowed searching for a solution.

A quick text to Mandie confirmed she was in the same conundrum. She couldn't use her data forager to crawl the internet looking for not-as-accessible information stores without more specific identifying information about Isabel. For now, Isabel Garcia was a ghost.

"She obviously reacted to the turkey sketch," I stated between bites of hash browns, now lukewarm, but at least still crispy and salty.

"What do we think that means?" Dan asked.

"She was quick to say that exonerated Lechuza. I'm inclined to agree with her since owls and turkeys do not resemble each other." I frowned around my coffee cup while I took a quick sip.

"It seems too easy?"

"I don't know if *easy* is the right word, but it does seem odd." I ticked off the steps in the case. "Isabel hired us because she suspected a supernatural component to the disappearances. Given the level of energy pouring off her, I believe she at least knows something about the supernatural world."

"Why hire us and then keep things from us?" Dan asked, drumming his hands on his dark blue jeans.

"Why tell us the rumor is that a Lechuza is responsible and then just roll with, yep, it's just a rumor?" I answered with my own question.

"Could it be that she somehow knows a Lechuza is not responsible, but needs help to figure out what the supernatural component is?"

I nodded at the supposition. "That's not a bad theory. And now that we've most likely ruled out a Lechuza, we're clear to find the real supernatural culprit."

"It still doesn't answer why she's keeping things from us," Dan pointed out.

"No, it does not," I agreed, remembering the cellphone from last night. "I'd like to know who she called as she was leaving our meeting." I'd put the detective's number in my phone the night before, so I made quick work of reaching out.

"This is Detective Snyder," he answered, sounding harried and stressed.

A feeling of dread stole over me. Since I needed physical proximity for my clairempathy, I knew the strong emotion was mine. His tone suggested something bad had happened and I worried it related to my case. "Good morning, Detective. This is Doctor Danger, from yesterday. Is now a bad time?"

"There's been some new developments," he answered vaguely. "Do you have something for me since yesterday?"

His curt tone, so different from before, threw me. Something was up. Instead of pushing, I tried giving a little to get a little. "Yes," I told him, then summarized our meeting with Isabel Garcia—not mentioning she was the client, of course—and ending with her phoning someone seconds after she left.

"Who is Isabel Garcia? How is she related to the investigation?" the detective asked in confusion.

I swore under my breath and then borrowed a page from his playbook. "Someone besides your deputy overheard my interview at the coffeeshop and mentioned it to her. She reached out to say she had information about the case."

"Did she have information?"

"Not really," I hedged my answer. "That's why I'm calling."

"You are?"

"Yes," I said, a hint of annoyance surfacing before I remembered that something must have happened for him to be this distracted. "Since she made a phone call after leaving our interview, I thought maybe you could get a warrant to pull her phone records."

Silence on the other end told me he was considering my suggestion. That he didn't dismiss it out of hand told me further that my hunch about Isabel knowing more than she let on was almost certainly accurate.

"Under normal circumstances, that wouldn't remotely be enough for a warrant," he began.

"But?"

He sighed. "Last night, Kimberly Roberts never came home from her evening jog."

"What?" I said, louder than I'd intended. Dan raised his eyebrows in question. "What happened?" I asked, then tilted the phone away from my ear so that Dan could also hear the detective's response, but nobody else in the sparsely-filled dining area could.

"Kimberly's parents called 9-1-1 at midnight to report their daughter missing. According to them, she went out for a jog around 8 pm and never returned."

"She doesn't live with them. How would they know so precisely?"

"According to her mother," he said. "Kimberly asked if she could stay with them for a couple of days."

"She was that worried about what had happened?"

"That would appear to be the case."

"It looks like she wasn't wrong. I assume none of her friends have seen her?" I asked.

"Not according to the parents, although, of course, we'll follow up with our interviews."

"Why the wait until midnight to call?" I asked.

"Short answer. They didn't think they could report her missing yet since not enough time had passed."

"The oft-repeated 24 hours. What prompted the call sooner than that then?"

"One of Kimberly's friend's parents assured them they didn't have to wait."

"Ah, okay. Anything else?" I asked.

"Isn't that enough?"

"That's fair," I said with a chuckle. "Because of this, can you pull Isabel's phone records?"

"I plan to ask," he assured me, "since Kimberly vanished after your chat with Isabel Garcia and her subsequent phone call."

Guilt flared painfully. Was this our fault for showing Isabel the police artist's sketch? Instead of asking that unanswerable question, I checked in with the detective, "Do you mind if I speak with Kimberly's parents and some of their neighbors?"

"Would anything I say stop you from doing so?" he replied, but I heard the smile in his voice.

"Not really," I quipped, trying and failing to lessen my remorse for my potential role in putting Kimberly back in the crosshairs.

He barked a laugh before sobering. "You have my unofficial blessing, as long as you tell me what you find."

I'll find Kimberly Roberts, I vowed to myself. I'd do anything to undo the damage.

CHAPTER NINE

The detective had been kind enough to provide Kimberly Roberts' parents' address. After quickly wrapping up breakfast, Dan drove our rental along Kemp Boulevard toward Lake Wichita. Soon he maneuvered the sedan beyond the driveway and parallel parked on the street in front of the house.

"Do you think they're home on a workday?" Dan asked after we exited the car.

"I hope so," I responded, taking in the healthy yard with bluebonnets and daisies blooming along the front of the single-story brick home. "We'll find out soon enough." I strode up the concrete driveway to the front door and pushed the bell. The classic ding-dong chime still echoed when someone pulled the light-brown door open.

"Yes?" the woman standing within the home asked with an air of desperation.

"Lisa Roberts?" I asked.

Her appearance left little doubt. She was an older version of her daughter, although she'd kept her brown hair, not dyed it blond like Kimberly. The laugh lines around her mouth and crow's feet around her eyes suggested a woman who liked to smile. At least under normal circumstances.

"I'm Lisa," she confirmed. "How may I help you?"

I held out a business card. "My name is Doctor Sarah Danger, and this is my associate, Daniel Trawl."

"Doctor Danger?" she asked in confusion. "Is this a joke?" A tremor of anger reverberated under the questions.

"No, ma'am. We are so sorry to intrude at a time like this. Detective Brad Snyder gave us your address. We're consulting on your daughter's missing persons case. May we speak with you?"

My overtly professional words and tone did the trick, and the simmering anger cooled. "Of course." Lisa stepped to the side of the door and gestured. "Please come inside. We can talk in the living room."

Dan and I entered the immaculate home, following our hostess across the luxury faux-wood flooring. The open floor plan meant that we could see from the beige sectional sofa in the living room to the kitchen behind a half-wall, as well as the backyard through glass doors flanking the fireplace along the far wall.

Lisa Roberts sat on one end of the sofa, watching us as we took seats on the other end. She wore white sneakers, purple leggings, and a lilac tunic with wide sleeves. Her red-rimmed eyes were the only indicator that something was amiss. Well, that and the worry, despair, and guilt pouring off of her. A squat jar candle glowed on the coffee table before us; I doubted the effectiveness of its calming scent of lavender. Thankfully, her emotional energy didn't appear to be supernaturally enhanced, and it bounced off my wall of protection. I made a note of the emotions and focused on my questions.

"Thank you so much—" I started to say before she jumped in.

"I'm not sure why Detective Snyder sent you. What kind of consultant are you?"

The question was benign, but I'd need to tread with care. Not everyone was open to the idea of the supernatural. "I run a consulting service to help individuals with more challenging situations," I responded vaguely; even my business card conveyed the most basic of information. The fact was that I'd never gotten my private investigator license. I was content to operate as a consultant. Most of our clients felt the same. Of course, Lisa Roberts wasn't a client.

Her forehead wrinkled. "Who hired you? How were you brought in so quickly? Why were you brought in?" Lisa's tone rose with each question, as did the intensity of her emotions bombarding my protection wall.

I took a slow, steadying breath before sidestepping the core of her questions. "We were technically brought in before you reported your daughter missing, but we believe—"

"I don't understand," Lisa interrupted again. "Billy—that's my husband—and I, of course, will take all the help we can get to bring our daughter home. But, I don't understand why the police brought in a consultant. You're here to do... what?"

"We sometimes see angles that others don't," I sidestepped again, then jumped in with a question of my own to redirect the conversation. "I know you've reviewed this with the police, but would you mind taking us through the events of last night?"

Lisa slumped back against the couch. "Kim said she wanted to take a quick jog after dinner. She lives downtown now, so she doesn't often get to see the lake," Lisa offered as an explanation. "Her father and I didn't want her to go. Despite what people said, we knew she wasn't drunk the night of the incident."

"How were you so confident?" I asked.

"She and I both have an aversion to alcohol. More than a drink will make us feel terrible." Lisa shook her head. "No, there's no way she was drunk."

"How do you explain what she says she saw?" I asked.

Lisa peered at me as if checking for nonverbal signs of my intention.

"I don't disbelieve her," I said gently. "That's part of why my team and I are here. To better understand what happened."

Lisa visibly relaxed for a moment before sitting upright and thinning her lips into a line. "I don't know. A trick of the light? Someone in a costume? Something… else?" Her pause before the final word piqued my curiosity.

"What did Kimberly tell you? When we spoke to her—"

"You spoke to Kim? When? Yesterday?" Lisa interrupted again, leaning forward eagerly. "What did she tell you? Had she seen anything else? Anyone else?" Her rapid-fire verbal approach was exhausting. I also picked up an increase in the level of guilt she was experiencing.

"She told us what she believes she saw that night outside the bar," I began, watching her physical reaction. "She didn't mention anyone or anything else. Is there some reason she might have?"

Lisa reddened. She picked at her fingers, resolutely not looking at me.

I waited, knowing she needed to be comfortable if she was going to tell me whatever she was withholding.

She stared at me with wide eyes before the words rushed out. "What if it was a hallucination that night? What if she wasn't kidnapped? What if she ran away? What if she's lost? Scared?" By the end of her torrent of words, I had to strain to hear her, but her guilt and grief relayed their way from her lips to my heart.

"Does Kimberly have a history of mental health issues?" I asked in a quiet voice.

"No…"

"But?"

"But she's graduating this semester, and she's been worried."

"About what?"

Lisa shrugged. "What all new graduates worry about, I suppose. Life. Paying for life."

"What do you mean?" I asked, trying to clarify if Kimberly had typical worries, or something more. That was an enormous leap from *worrying about life after graduation* to *hallucinating a man-size turkey trying to kidnap me.*

"She hadn't lined up a job for after graduation, and I know she was worried about what she would do if she couldn't get one before she graduated."

"Have you seen any recent changes in her behavior?" I asked, probing the mental health angle further.

After some thought, Lisa shook her head.

"Any reason to think that she ran off last night?" I tried again for a careful tone.

Lisa sighed. "No." She laughed ruefully. "The idea that she just ran away to get away feels like the lesser of the two evils when compared to the idea that someone might have kidnapped her," she admitted. "But…"

"But?"

Tears filled and overflowed her eyes. She blinked several times to stem the tide, before brushing the backs of her hands furiously against her cheeks. "If she was struggling that much… and I missed it… didn't get her the help she needed," Lisa whispered the last words. "What kind of mother would I be?"

A crest of guilt slammed into my internal barrier from Lisa about her perception that she might have failed to protect her daughter. Combined with my guilt that my presence and interview of the young lady put her back in harm's way, I blinked back my own tears.

Lisa reached out a hand to take mine. Ironic, I supposed. "Are you okay?" she asked.

"Yes," I choked out. "I'm just feeling especially close to this investigation." Those were the wrong words to say.

"Why?" She released my hand and cooly stared at me. "Why would you feel especially close to this investigation? Who are you?" She leaned forward to grab her cellphone off the coffee table in front of the sofa.

At first, I thought she was maybe going to call the detective to confirm my identity. When she started jabbing at the phone's keyboard, I figured out what she was doing, and tried to head her off. "Lisa, let me explain my specialty."

"Supernatural specialist? You're a supernatural specialist? And a clairempath? What even is that?" Her voice had risen an octave. "The police are okay with this?"

"Yes, I am, and yes, they are," I soothed, trying to stop her rising incredulity that was spiraling to anger. She had needed a target to vent her whirlwind of emotions, and I'd just become it.

"Let me guess. You believe a giant bird almost kidnapped her. Right?" The derision in her voice cut like glass.

"We are still working on a viable theory," I began, but she cut me off one last time.

"I don't know what your end game is," she bit off, "but I'd like you both to leave." Lisa jumped to her feet and stalked to her front door.

Dan and I scrambled to follow her. I stumbled from the disorientation caused by her maelstrom of anger, guilt, and fear swirling around me.

The strength of the fear hit me the most. We mumbled our apologies as we left. I didn't take it personally when Lisa slammed the door behind us. She wasn't mad at us. And she wasn't dismissing the possibility.

She was terrified that we were right.

CHAPTER TEN

Dan waited for me to decide our next step. I stood beside our rental car, scanning the surrounding road.

"None of what Lisa Roberts told us changes the plan," I stated. "The last time Kimberly was seen was heading out for a nighttime jog. It's time to canvass the neighborhood."

"Have the police spoken to anyone yet?" Dan asked.

"Not that the detective mentioned. If not, I'm sure it's on their list for today." I shaded my eyes as I looked back the way we had come. "Let's start this way—" I pointed in the opposite direction, toward the lake. "—since Kimberly's mom said she liked to jog that area." This part of the neighborhood had short roads with houses nearer to each other. Depending on how far she'd jogged, she may have passed quite a few of them. They were larger, in different shades of classic Texas brick, with well-manicured lawns. The neighborhood was quiet at this time of the day. I suspected a fair number of people would still be at work, but maybe we'd get lucky.

We didn't get lucky at the first house. Or the second or the third. Nobody was home. Until finally, the door to the fourth home swung open in response to our ringing the doorbell.

"Good afternoon," I said to the balding, middle-aged man who had answered the door.

"I'm not interested," he interrupted me, turning away.

"We're here on behalf of the police," I hurriedly added, and miracle of miracles, it worked.

The man stopped closing the door and squinted his brown eyes at me. "Are you looking for donations?"

"No, sir," I answered before explaining our purpose. His mouth turned down when I finished.

"Kim's a good kid," the man told us, "but I didn't see her yesterday. Hopefully, the alert will bring someone forward who did."

"Alert?" Dan asked.

"The alert on the neighborhood app," the man explained.

"What did the alert say and who posted it?" I asked.

"It was from someone in the police department who just asked if anybody in the area had seen Kim since last night. There were already several comments under the alert, but none that I saw with any real information." He shook his head. "I'm sorry that I can't be more help."

"When did you see the alert?" I followed up.

"I saw it when I got up this morning. Since I work from home, though, I don't get up until nine, so it could have come in earlier and I wouldn't have noticed."

I started to thank him for his time and then stopped. "Have you looked at the alert since this morning?"

"No, I haven't."

"Do you mind checking it again so we can see if there were any additional comments that might be helpful?"

"Of course," he agreed, pulling his phone from his back pocket. He unlocked the screen and we watched him find the app and open it before handing the phone to me.

I tilted it so Dan could see as I confirmed that the police did, in fact, issue the alert early that morning, and then I summarized the comments under the alerts. "Mostly people expressing their concern for Kimberly or offering prayers for her quick return." I closed the app and handed him his phone. "That's it. You're correct that it doesn't appear anyone saw anything."

We thanked him for his time, and he closed the door as we turned away.

"That's helpful to know the police issued an alert as soon as Kimberly's parents called," Dan said while we walked back to the sidewalk, "but unfortunate that nobody saw anything."

"At least nobody who commented on the alert," I corrected him.

"True," he agreed.

The next several houses combined a variety of disappointing outcomes. Either nobody was home or they didn't see anything and hoped the police found Kimberly safe. After an hour, we'd finished that small cluster of roads and had moved into the neighboring community, frustration building.

"I hope this isn't fruitless," I muttered, the passage of time haunting me. Dusk had arrived and street lights popped on. "I'd have thought more people would have been home by now."

"It's also possible they're simply not answering the door," Dan said.

I sighed. "Yeah, that's a good point. If we don't find someone soon, we may have to stop for the night."

"For sure. Once it's dinnertime, people will dislike our interruptions even more."

I surveyed the road ahead. "There are five houses around this cul-de-sac. Let's do these and then we'll call it."

Dan agreed and we continued. Ringing the doorbells elicited answers at the first three, but our hope was short-lived as the homeowners repeated what we'd heard thus far.

We stood at the door of a smaller, single-story home with a bright red door. The doorbell had just finished tolling when the door opened to reveal a taller, middle-aged woman.

"Hello?" she asked uncertainly when she saw us.

I wondered if we surprised her because someone else was expected, but rushed ahead with my explanation of who we were and why we were there. When I reached the statement about working with the police, she interrupted.

"Is this about the missing girl from the alert?" she asked, a spike of worry pinging off of my protection wall.

"Yes," I answered. "Did you see something?"

"Not directly," she said, and my heart fell, "but when I saw the alert on social media, I checked my security camera."

"Was something there?" Dan asked.

"Maybe," she hedged. "I saw a woman matching the missing girl's description. It caught my eye in part because she was having an animated conversation with another woman."

Excitement swelled. Finally! New information. Then I focused on the specific words the woman had used. "Animated? Was it an argument?" I asked, my interest piqued, along with my concern about who Kimberly might have been speaking to.

"I couldn't say."

"What made it animated?" I asked instead.

"You know. Talking with their hands, gesturing at each other and around them. Definitely animated."

"Did your video pick up what they were talking about?"

"Not from that distance, no."

"Where were they standing?" I asked, turning to peer back at the sidewalk. It would be a pretty clear view. No large vegetation or anything blocking the camera's sightline.

The woman pointed toward the street. "They were in the street, not on the sidewalk. That's a big issue in the neighborhood," she added as an aside, "joggers using the road instead of the sidewalk at night. Very dangerous."

I murmured my agreement. "May we see the footage?"

"Of course," she agreed. "Come on in. My phone is back in the kitchen."

Dan and I followed the woman through a neutrally-designed home to a small kitchen at the back. Well-maintained, but not updated since its original build, likely in the 80s. I idly wondered if she'd inherited it. She grabbed her phone off the tile countertop.

"Apologies, ma'am," I began before she started searching for the video. "What did you say your name was?" She hadn't identified herself, but we had jumped so quickly into her footage that Dan and I forgot to ask after introducing ourselves.

"Jessica Faber," she belatedly introduced herself. She offered an amused smile as we shook hands.

"It's nice to meet you, even under these circumstances," I added. "Thank you for inviting us into your home and for helping."

Jessica's smile crinkled the edges of her blue eyes. "Of course. Anything I can do to help." She returned her attention to the phone, poking the screen and scrolling until she found what she wanted. She turned the phone toward us and hit play.

My heart fell as the women came into focus. I recognized both of them. Kimberly Roberts, wearing a light-colored fitted shirt over old-school loose jogging shorts, stood almost nose-to-nose with another woman.

That woman, not dressed for jogging in her jeans and a flowing top, flipped her long curly hair over a shoulder. Isabel Garcia.

With Dan and Jessica standing on either side of me, we watched the silent pantomime. I understood what Jessica meant by animated. First Isabel, and then Kim, gesticulated rather energetically, though it appeared both intended to emphasize points. They didn't appear to be gesturing toward each other or pointing toward anything. I agreed with Jessica's assessment: animated but not an argument.

But what were they talking about?

Before I could voice my rhetorical question, the video reached its end. Our third victim, Kimberly Roberts, jogged away from Isabel, who stared after her for a beat, before striding away in the opposite direction.

The three of us remained silent until the two women left the screen.

"Did you show this to the police?" I asked, handing the phone back to Jessica.

"Absolutely. As soon as I saw the footage. That's her, right? The missing college student?" The worry carried through her tone, bouncing harder off my internal barrier. My stomach clenched with shared anxiousness, the bitter taste of bile rising in my throat. I inhaled the clean scent inside Jessica's home and focused on relaxing before responding.

"Yes, it is," I concurred. "Thank you so much for checking your footage. This is very helpful."

"I'm so glad. I hope she's found safe," Jessica added, rubbing a cross on a gold chain around her neck.

"The police are doing everything they can," I responded by rote, though I meant every word.

"That's not all I saw," she blurted out. I heard hesitation in her voice.

"It's not?" I asked.

"I don't know if the fog is relevant."

"Fog?" Dan asked before I could.

Jessica nodded. "After I saw that discussion, I fast-forwarded through all of the video my security camera captured last night. It didn't take long to see the fog." She'd been speaking while scrolling and tilted the phone so that Dan and I could view the screen again. It was paused on the empty scene of the roadway and sidewalk, lit by a nearby streetlight.

The video played forward. A pillowy fog undulated across the bottom of the screen, almost like the tail end of a bigger blanket of fog offscreen. It seeped around the tree on the strip of grass between the sidewalk and road, growing denser as it filled up more of the screen. After several minutes, the fog dissipated as if burned off by the morning sun, even though it was still nighttime.

Kimberly, Dan, and I held silent for a beat after the video's conclusion.

"I assume no identifiable sounds on that one either?" I broke the silence.

"Unfortunately, no, still too far away," Jessica said. "Do you think it's related?"

"I have absolutely no idea," I admitted.

"I wasn't sure if I should show it to you."

"You didn't show that to the police," I guessed.

Her cheeks colored. "I didn't want to look stupid," she said, staring at the floor while she put her phone in a back pocket.

"At this point," I told her, placing one hand on her forearm to pull her attention, "we don't know what information is relevant. That fog certainly appeared unusual, so it's worth sharing."

"I mean, we do get fog," she said in a rush, backtracking, "including at night. It might not mean anything."

"Let us worry about figuring out if it's significant."

Jessica nodded. "Thank you."

"Let us know if you see or hear anything else unusual," I said, handing her my card. "We'll let the police know about the rolling fog," I concluded the interview.

After saying our goodbyes, Dan and I walked back to the rental car in silence, the growing darkness surrounding us. Once seated in the sedan, I spoke after he slid the key into the ignition.

"Time to speak to Isabel."

CHAPTER ELEVEN

A quick internet search found The Parkway Grill for a local casual-dining option. The restaurant had framed posters on the walls, flags hanging from the ceiling, and several televisions tuned to sports stations. The smell of fried onion rings hit me and my stomach growled.

"Guess you'll need some food," Dan joked.

"You heard that?"

"I think everyone heard that." He chuckled, then nodded toward a woman—hostess or waitress—who hustled over to us.

"Table for two?" she asked.

"Three," I answered, then pointed past the open area of the restaurant to an empty booth in a back corner. It was situated under a television, but the sound seemed off, so I thought it was a good choice.

"I'll be right there with menus and water," she replied and hustled away.

"Thank you," I called after her before Dan and I walked to the booth. I slid across the maroon seat, facing the door so I could watch for Isabel's arrival. Dan sat opposite me. We didn't have to wait long.

"Here she comes," I told him when I saw Isabel scanning the restaurant for us. My call to Isabel had gone almost exactly as I expected, including that she did not sound surprised by my request to meet.

Isabel's appearance shocked me. She seemed to have aged overnight, with dark bags under her brown eyes. Frowning chapped lips accentuated deep wrinkles, lending a ragged look. She slumped onto the booth bench next to Dan and her tired eyes met my inquisitive ones.

I wasn't sure what was going on with Isabel, but removing a stone from my wall of protection gave me a clue. A mild wave of supernatural energy brushed against my mind. It wasn't threatening or aggressive. Just tired, if it was possible for supernatural energy to be tired.

"Are you okay, Isabel?" I asked.

Isabel stifled a sigh. "I didn't sleep well."

Dan and I waited for her to continue.

Isabel remained silent.

The waitress arrived with three menus and three glasses of water. Isabel jumped at the diversion and dove into the menu. My growling stomach reminded me that I was hungry.

"What do you recommend?" I asked the waitress.

"We're known for our cheese sticks, and depending on how hungry you are, you can get those for the table plus burgers and onion rings," she answered.

That sounded deliciously decadent. After confirming our orders, the waitress left and we turned our attention to Isabel, who stayed stubbornly silent.

"Why didn't you sleep well?" I asked directly.

"I'm worried," she whispered, her fingers fidgeting where they sat clasped on the tabletop.

"About what?"

"About… about what's happening."

"What's happening?"

Isabel stared at her fidgeting fingers.

"Did anything happen yesterday that you'd like to tell us about?" I asked.

Again, Isabel did not answer, though worry arose in her energy, lapping again at my protection wall.

A glance at Dan confirmed the lack of answers frustrated him, too. It was time to bring out the big guns, so to speak.

"We saw a very interesting video earlier today," I stated with a deliberate lack of detail.

Isabel's gaze jumped up to meet mine and she caught her breath, staring at me like the proverbial deer in headlights. "What video?"

"Security feed. From someone's house camera." My chest tightened following my answer, and I struggled to breathe.

Oh my god, she knows. How could she know? She knows.

Dan's concerned expression told me that I was broadcasting powerful emotions. Since I hadn't been experiencing anything—

It had to be Isabel. She'd dropped her head again to stare at the table, but her shoulders hitched as if she was crying or trying to catch her breath.

I closed my eyes and, with effort, turned my attention inward, visualizing my stone protective wall soaring to the heavens. My mind's eye saw dark, distrustful shades of black, red, and gray swirling around, trying to push their way through the small hole I'd created when I removed a single stone. Seeing paranormal emotions as colors was an unusual occurrence, though not without precedent. It highlighted just how much supernatural energy Isabel projected. I fought against the waves of emotions to replace the stone. The feelings dissipated. With a shaky breath of relief, I opened my eyes and stared at the crown of Isabel's head.

Isabel must be the source of this massive spike in negative supernatural energy. The predominant emotion was fear. While my crazed heartbeat settled, I considered what she could be afraid of. Getting caught was the most logical. And yet, that seemed off somehow. Besides, I debated with myself, why would she have sought my help if she was the one responsible?

"What are you afraid of?" I asked.

Isabel's head shot up. "Afraid of?"

"You heard me."

"I told you. I'm worried about what's been happening," she answered, strength returning to her voice.

"No," I disagreed. "You aren't just worried." I considered how hard to push. Given that there was another missing woman… I'd push pretty hard. "Remember why you hired me?"

"Yes," she whispered, her shoulders slumping.

I dropped my voice. "I feel your fear. It's overwhelming you, and will overwhelm me if I allow it."

"I'm sorry." Her eyes brimmed with tears.

"Don't apologize. Tell me what you're afraid I know."

"Wha-what are you talking about?"

"I don't know," I snapped, before calming myself. "During your massive supernatural outpouring, I interpreted that as you being afraid of me knowing something. What are you afraid of me knowing?"

"I don't know what you're talking about," she insisted, and I sensed her irritation with me. Now I wasn't sure how much of my irritation was hers or mine.

I chuckled, surprising Isabel and Dan.

"What's funny?" She bit off her question.

Before answering her, I took a chance and removed a stone from my wall to allow my abilities a moment to prepare prior to poking her again. "That you would hire me, only to withhold what likely is critical information. What are you worried that I know? You know I saw you and the victim—"

My over-enunciation of the word proved effective when she flinched.

"—on a neighbor's security video arguing." Okay, technically, I didn't think that was accurate. But Isabel didn't need to know that.

Now her face took on a sickly green cast.

"What were you arguing about?"

"Nothing. We weren't arguing," she snarled at me.

"She vanished after that conversation. What did you do to her?" I taunted her with my question. In a fit of tactical inspiration, I lobbed a verbal grenade. "What does the fog in the video mean?"

Isabel shot to her feet and I mirrored her. Dan rose, too, though his stance suggested it was more for protective purposes. Isabel and I glared at each other. Fear and anger swirled in my mind.

How dare she speak to me like this? If only she knew. I have to protect—

"Who do you have to protect, Isabel?"

Like water doused on a blazing fire, an emptiness overtook me, and those final, surprising thoughts splintered.

Isabel gave a curt shake of her head. "I have to go," she blurted out, then fled from the table, almost crashing into our waitress.

CHAPTER TWELVE

"Guess that leaves more for you two," the waitress quipped uneasily before placing our food on the table.

After the waitress withdrew, I answered Dan's unspoken questions. "Yes, she continues to have incredible amounts of supernatural energy. Yes, she is afraid of us finding out something. But, no, I don't think she's a kidnapper."

Dan quirked an eyebrow. "She just happens to be surrounded by supernatural energy and smack in the middle of our case?"

I shrugged. "I can't explain it. Yet."

"Who is it that Isabel is trying to protect?" Dan asked.

"Who said Isabel is trying to protect someone?" I asked in confusion.

"Um, you did?"

"I did?" A tendril of fear curled around my spine at the thought I wasn't remembering something that had just happened.

Dan frowned. "You did. About five minutes ago." Understanding dawned on his face. "It happened when Isabel's emotions overwhelmed you."

"Oh," I said, frantically searching my recollection. "I've never not remembered what happened during an episode."

"Not that you've ever reported," Dan agreed.

The tendril of fear became a vine of panic as confusion swamped me over the missing experience. And another sense of déjà vu rocked me. Had this happened before? But wouldn't Dan remember my telling him about it if it did?

"What can I do?"

Dan's matter-of-fact question stopped the spiraling negative thoughts and emotions. "You just did it," I thanked him. Curiosity overtook the worry. "This is fascinating. I wonder what could cause me not to remember what I experienced."

"Isabel must have some high levels of supernatural energy, right?"

"Either that or she's been around someone with off-the-charts supernatural energy. Although my gut tells me there's almost zero chance she's getting that level of energy secondhand."

"What now?" Dan asked.

"Let's check in with Detective Snyder, now that we know the police released a social media alert for Kimberly."

I glanced at my rapidly cooling food. The delectable smell had faded with the food's heat and although I imagined the savory flavor on my tongue, I was sad that it looked like I wouldn't get to eat.

"Maybe they've gotten some new information?"

"We also can see if they got a search warrant to pull her phone records." I withdrew my cellphone from my backpack and autodialed the detective, who picked up on the first ring.

"Doc Danger, how are you on this fine Texas evening?" he drawled.

"We're great, Detective," I responded. "I was calling to see if you were able to pull Isabel's phone records and if you've gotten any responses to your social media alert."

"You saw it?" Detective Snyder asked, sounding surprised, and not answering my first question.

"Yes," I answered. "Plus, several neighbors reported seeing it when we canvassed the third victim's parents' neighborhood this afternoon."

"Did you learn anything?"

I chuckled. Classic police technique. "I'll show you mine if you show me yours," I teased and a booming laugh sounded in my ears.

"Touché, Doc, touché. I'll go first," he offered. "It's quick. To answer your first question, the judge denied our request for the phone records. That was a long-shot, so not surprising. To answer your second question, so far, only one neighbor reported seeing anything. And she didn't see it firsthand."

"Security footage?" I interrupted to ask.

"How did you know?"

"I'm guessing we spoke to your lone source since she told us she showed the police the same footage she showed us."

"Hmm, okay," he said. "That would be unfortunate. I would have liked more evidence."

"That makes sense. To be clear, you received footage from Jessica Faber?" I asked. "She showed us footage of two incidents of note."

"That would be our lone source," he confirmed. "Wait. You said two incidents?"

"In addition to the animated conversation she told us she showed you or one of your officers, she also showed us an unusual weather pattern."

"Unusual weather pattern? What on earth are you talking about?"

I described the fog that rolled in to fill the screen and then back out, but that seemed part of a larger whole offscreen.

"How is that relevant to the case?" he asked in a bewildered tone.

"I'm not sure," I admitted. "Something about it looked unnatural."

"I'll make a note of it," he said, "but I'm not sure how to follow that up."

"Don't worry," I said. "We plan to do so." Although I hoped he didn't ask how, since I had no real idea.

"Ms. Faber recognized Kimberly Roberts from our alert," the detective switched to the section of the footage with the obvious connection to the missing persons case, "but unfortunately, she didn't recognize the other woman in the security video."

I hesitated a moment before responding. "I do."

"You what? Recognize the woman that the kidnap victim is speaking with in the video?" The detective's voice had sharpened with interest.

"We don't know for certain that Kimberly has been kidnapped," I pointed out.

"Do you recognize the woman that the missing person is speaking with in the video? Is that better?" The detective managed to keep most of his apparent irritation out of his revised question.

My face flushed. "Apologies. Habit."

A small sigh sounded. "It's fine. Do you know her or not?"

"Yes, I do." I experienced one more moment of hesitation before deciding that the three missing college students might need a faster solution. "It's Isabel Garcia."

"Wait. That's the woman whose phone records you wanted pulled." Silence as he either searched his memory banks or, more likely, thumbed through his case notes. "She's also the one you said reached out to you when she overheard you at the coffeeshop."

"Yes, she lives here in Wichita Falls," I said.

"Who is she really? How do you know her?"

"I met her in Dallas."

"In Dallas? How did you meet in Dallas?" he interrupted.

"I was at a convention and she found me there."

"She found you?"

"If you'll stop interrupting," I pointed out, "I can give you the pertinent information."

"Of course," he said with a soft chuckle. "Please, continue."

I explained how Isabel Garcia tracked me down at the annual meeting of the National Association of Detectives, appearing during the awards banquet. I chose to leave out the high levels of supernatural energy she seemed to emit.

"This is the woman who hired you," he stated rather than asked. "Not just a random woman who overheard you interviewing Kimberly Roberts in the coffeeshop."

"Excellent deduction, Detective."

"That's why they pay me the big bucks."

"Isabel is involved somehow," I said, "but I truly don't think she's responsible for the college students disappearing."

"Why not?" he asked. "You asked me to pull her phone records."

"Why would she have hired me to find the individual responsible?"

"I don't need to point out to you how often guilty parties insinuate themselves into investigations, do I?"

I exhaled noisily. "No, you don't."

"You believe she's involved, but not responsible. I ask again, why not?" He continued before I could answer. "Is it from your ability?"

"Something like that, yes."

"We'll talk to her," he stated, then ended the conversation.

I relayed the detective's side of the conversation to Dan and then reconsidered my food. I needed to eat, but my appetite had waned in response to what I'd disclosed. It had felt necessary to be forthcoming with the detective. I stood behind my choice.

So why did I feel such a sense of foreboding, like I'd set something terrible in motion?

CHAPTER THIRTEEN

My roiling stomach and shortness of breath awoke me the next morning. I flip-flopped back and forth over my decision to tell the detective Isabel's identity while I brushed my teeth, showered, and dressed for the day. My uncertainty led me to call a different number than Dan.

"Peanut, you have great timing. I'm between patients," Dr. Stephanie Danger, my clairempath veterinarian mother, greeted me. Of course, she used my permanently affixed childhood nickname. As if being the only one in the family who got the short gene wasn't bad enough. I smiled at her voice, knowing she knew I secretly loved the nickname.

"Did I tell you I'm in Texas?"

"Still?" she asked in surprise. "Isn't the convention over?"

"Let me catch you up." After updating her on the details of the case, I brought up the crux of my current distress. "If my interview resulted in Kimberly Roberts' kidnapping—"

"A big if," my mother interrupted.

"—and something happens now to Isabel because I told the police I recognized her on the video?" I continued as if she hadn't interrupted.

"Did you make the best decision you could in the moment with the information available to you at that time?" my mother asked.

"I believe so."

"Did you do so in good faith with the express purpose of finding the missing college students?"

"I did," I asserted, beginning to feel better. Moms were so good for that.

"And, finally, you know that the fact that you feel guilty—" Way to hit the nail on the head, Mom. "—is because you care. You care about the missing college students and you care about your client. You can only do the best you can do."

"Thanks, Mom."

"Anytime, Peanut." She laughed as barking overtook her voice. "I've gotta go. Talk soon."

After disconnecting the call, I resolutely landed on believing I did the right thing. Then my belief reversed again when I texted Dan to meet me downstairs for breakfast. My mind swirled anew as I made my way to the dining room. The uncertainty about my decision apparently planned to stick with me.

"Didn't sleep well?" he asked.

"That's a great way to greet someone and tell them they look bad," I responded with a smirk.

"You know I always think you look good," he replied and waggled his eyebrows, continuing his ongoing innocent flirtation that he knew I'd ignore. I'd established that we would remain friends from the beginning of our relationship. But I'd be lying if I said I didn't enjoy our flirtations.

The uneasiness regarding my decision to tell the detective about Isabel hit me again.

"Hey, you know I'm just teasing," Dan hurried to add, concern showing in his hazel eyes behind frameless glasses.

"What?" I asked, before realizing what he meant. I waved a hand at him. "You know I don't care about that." I bit my lower lip. "I'm having second thoughts about having told Detective Snyder about Isabel hiring us."

His brow wrinkled. "Why? It makes sense to stay all hands on deck until the missing students are found."

I sighed and leaned back in my chair. "Intellectually, I know that. Emotionally, there's just this sense…" My sentence trailed off. "I even called my mother this morning."

"Then how could you possibly still doubt your choices," Dan said with a smile. "Your mother is almost as brilliant as you."

"Thanks." I tried to match his smile.

"How would you feel if another student disappeared?" he asked in a somber tone.

"Quit being so reasonable," I grumbled good-naturedly, knowing he was right and only repeating back to me what my brain had played on repeat all night. And what my mother would have told me if I hadn't agreed with her so quickly.

"Let's grab our food and then we can talk it through," he suggested.

Since I hadn't eaten much the night before, my stomach chose that moment to growl in agreement. We rose and headed to the buffet. Not everyone loved these assembly-line breakfasts, but I didn't mind them. They were easy, and you had your pick between basic, but filling, food like bagels, cereal, and even eggs or pancakes.

Back at the table, Dan helped me talk through my mixed feelings about my disclosure, and I at last squished down the uneasy feeling that didn't want to leave. I savored the scent of my mug of house-blend coffee to aid in calming my nerves. Just as I lifted the cup to my lips for a sip, my cellphone rang and a face popped up on my screen.

"Good morning, Mandie," I greeted her after answering the call. A glance around the room confirmed that we had it to ourselves that morning. "Let me put you on speaker."

"Hi, Mandie," Dan called out.

"Hey team," she responded. "How much do you love me?"

I grinned. "With all the love in the world. What did you find?"

"Isabel Garcia was a hard woman to track down," she began. "At first, it appeared she just materialized out of thin air in college."

"New identity?" I interrupted to ask.

"You'd think that, right? But, no. It turns out that she was in foster care with her younger brother."

"Child services would have sealed those records. How did you find them?"

"I didn't, actually, despite my best efforts," she admitted. "Social media provided the information, believe it or not."

"How?"

"An El Paso Police Department report on a deadly house fire that left two teenaged orphans."

"El Paso?"

"My forager found the reference," Mandie said with pride. Her internet forager was the stuff of legend on our team. She could find anything in the public record, and even get behind quite a number of firewalls. On those occasions, I was glad I wasn't officially a private investigator with a license to risk.

"Isabel and her brother?" I asked.

"It would appear so. I couldn't find anything on the brother after high school. He's a dead end at this point."

"I'll ask Isabel about him when I see her, if only to rule out any involvement." I drank more coffee. "And Isabel?"

"I found references to that name at a half dozen different high schools."

"We established the name Isabel Garcia isn't super unique. Those surely weren't all her."

"No, they weren't," Mandie confirmed. "But I believe at least three of them are."

"Which would suggest moving around, which would suggest changing foster homes?" I followed her logic. "How did you conclude they were her?"

I heard the glee in her voice when she answered. "Because of what else my forager found mentioned by students at those schools."

"Don't keep us in suspense," Dan called out.

"References to sightings of Lechuza," Mandie finished triumphantly.

I gasped at the revelation. My mind raced to make sense of this new piece of information and I spoke my thoughts out loud. "If Isabel is a Lechuza, that would explain the tremendous amounts of supernatural energy I feel around her. Why would she have hired me? Could she believe it's another Lechuza? Or that a Lechuza is not responsible for the missing college students? But, if not a Lechuza, what are the odds there's another supernatural being in tiny Wichita Falls?"

Dan spoke when I stopped to breathe. "Maybe we need to reconsider whether there's a supernatural component to this case. Just to rule it out."

"Is it possible these college students ran away of their own volition; were taken or hurt by a non-supernatural person or persons; or, the cases are unrelated?" Mandie asked, and I could practically hear her ticking these three options off on her fingers while she spoke.

"Let's pause a moment on all the speculating," I said, trying to slow everything down. "I haven't even put you on the trail of the unusual weather patterns yet."

"The unusual weather patterns?" Mandie asked, interest piqued.

I explained what we'd seen on the security footage.

"Got it, boss. I'll set the forager looking for mentions of unusual weather patterns, specifically fog, on the nights the other two women went missing."

"Thanks, Mandie. Regarding the other new information," I said, bringing us back around. "Are we jumping to conclusions about Isabel being a Lechuza? What are the odds it's a coincidence that there were reported Lechuza sightings in connection to three high schools where we found the name Isabel Garcia?"

"I can answer that," Mandie offered.

"You have the floor," I told her.

"Okay, I don't have the exact statistics—though I could get them if you wanted—but I found almost zero references in the same timeframe anywhere else in El Paso during the times I found them at those three high schools connected to Isabel Garcia."

"That's not conclusive, but it's intriguing," I concluded.

"What's the next step, boss?" Mandie asked.

"It's time for a no-holds-barred conversation with Isabel Garcia."

CHAPTER FOURTEEN

Our plan fizzled when Isabel Garcia failed to answer her phone. My follow-up text expressing our urgent need to speak with her garnered no response.

"Okay, what's the next, next step, boss?" Dan asked, mimicking Mandie's earlier question.

I considered our options. Mandie was still trying to find more information on Isabel, her vanished-in-the-wind brother, and the unusual nighttime fog, but my big step was to confront Isabel with the hypothesis that she was a Lechuza. Her response would suggest the next avenues to consider, including her connection, or not, to the disappearing college students.

"How else can we find her?" I mused aloud. "We know she works for the Wichita Falls Independent School District. Do we know where and in what capacity? I thought Mandie's email mentioned English as a Second Language."

Dan leaned forward in his seat to withdraw his computer tablet from his backpack. His eyes moved back and forth as he scanned several documents, presumably also Mandie's email. "It looks like she might work as a translator within the school district."

"Hmm, so she's not tied to a specific school?"

"I don't believe so," he murmured, as he tapped at the screen. "Let me pop on the school district's website and see if I can find a contact number." A few more keystrokes and then he frowned.

"What is it?" I asked.

"It looks like there's a main number listed for most of their departments. It's either for their downtown facility or is like a switchboard. I doubt that if we call and ask where she is, they would tell us."

"No, probably not. Nor should they, to be honest." I ate a bite of room-temperature eggs and sighed dramatically.

"You need to learn to eat faster," Dan teased.

I resisted the temptation to toss a forkful of egg at him and gave him a broad smile.

"You have an idea?" he asked.

"Let's walk and talk," I instructed, rising from the table. Dan matched my movements, and we cleared our breakfast mess before exiting the dining area.

"Where are we going?" he asked as we reached the doors to the parking lot.

"We are taking a field trip to the school district's main office. They likely wouldn't give us any information over the phone; that's true. But, if we present our credentials in person, well, maybe that could be a different story."

Dan chuckled. "Our credentials?"

"I have a business card," I quipped. "You also have a fairly well-known blog."

"So I have the credentials," he said, striking a superhero pose for dramatic effect.

"Yes, you do," I said with a smirk as we buckled ourselves into the car.

Dan waited to back out until I had entered the location on Broad Street into my phone's mapping software. While we continued our conversation, he followed the mellow voice to our destination.

"What's our play?"

"I'm thinking we skirt pretty close to the truth. From what we've seen, folks are getting freaked out by three missing college students. If we namedrop Detective Brad Snyder and say we're working with him, I'm confident they'll be more forthcoming."

"Working with him is a bit of a stretch, no?"

I shrugged. "We're not working against him," I pointed out.

"True," Dan agreed. He pulled into a parking lot situated off Central Freeway and below an overpass, finding a parking spot practically in the shadow of the front door. Lettering above the door confirmed that the several-blocks-wide tan building was indeed the Wichita Falls Independent School District Education Center.

We strode toward the glass front doors, wind blowing my auburn hair around my face, and bathing me in a warm, spicy aroma. We drove past a taqueria a block earlier, I remembered, as I tucked strands of hair behind my ears. Both my thoughts and steps halted when a trace of curiosity and worry pulsed against my protection wall. Scanning the area around the building, I saw two women huddled next to a large metal bell on a concrete stand. Instead of entering the building, I altered course to the right to intercept them. Their emotions strengthened the closer Dan and I got. It was higher than expected for an office setting but not supernaturally enhanced. I suspected we wouldn't need to go far to find Isabel Garcia.

Surely she's not involved. We would have known.

I didn't know the source of the stray thoughts, but I doubted they were mine and suspected I knew the subject that prompted them.

The women, speaking in hushed tones, paused in their whispering as I approached with my hand extended.

"Good morning," I greeted the duo who were wearing standard business casual and distraught expressions. "My name is—"

"You aren't with the press, are you?" The tall redhead's question sounded inquisitory, not accusatory, but her scathing up and down glance told me what answer would end the conversation. Thankfully, I wouldn't even have to lie.

"No, I'm not," I answered, dropping my outstretched hand. "Has something happened?"

"We should be careful who we speak with," the older woman with a sleek gray bob and cracked lips in need of lip balm jumped in. She was clearly speaking to her colleague and not answering my question.

"My name is Doctor Sarah Danger," I tried again, and the *doctor* in my name seized their attention. "I'm looking for Isabel Garcia."

The older woman made the sign of the cross and the redhead's hand flew up to cover her mouth. These startled responses provided me with all the confirmation I needed of my hunch about the source of the swirling curiosity and worry.

"I'm working with Detective Brad Snyder of the Wichita Falls Police Department and need to know where she is today," I continued on smoothly, ignoring the muted chortle from Dan standing next to me.

The redhead squinted in response. "If you're working with the detective, then you should know where Isabel is."

My heart sank, but I soldiered on with my bluff. "The detective and I missed each other this morning," I lied, hopefully as smoothly. "Was he here?"

"Yes, Doctor Danger," the gray-haired older woman answered, earning a look of consternation from the redhead.

"Sherry!" the redhead admonished.

"Hush, Angie, maybe the doctor can answer some of our questions," Sherry retorted.

"A little quid pro quo, Sherry," I asked with a quirked eyebrow. I liked her.

"Why are you looking for Isabel?" Sherry asked.

"She asked for my help in locating the missing college students," I answered, leaving out that she was my client.

"See, Angie, I knew Isabel didn't do anything," Sherry said to her colleague, whose lips thinned in displeasure.

"Why would you think Isabel did something?" I asked, guilt surging anew that I'd given the detective Isabel's name.

The ladies exchanged a look before Angie answered. "That detective was here when we opened, asking to speak to Isabel. He had two uniformed officers with him."

"They arrested her," Sherry interrupted in a loud whisper.

"We don't know that," Angie contradicted.

"Did Isabel leave with the detective and the officers?" I asked, trying to clarify if law enforcement had indeed arrested my client.

"Detective Snyder said she just needed to come downtown to answer questions," Sherry said, before looking over the top of her thick black-framed glasses. "We all know what that means."

Angie nodded in agreement, adding, "We followed them out here and saw them put her in the back of a squad car."

"She wouldn't have asked you for help if she was guilty. Would she?" Sherry asked, her voice quavering.

"I don't believe so," I said.

"We don't think she's involved either," Angie stated, but I sensed her undercurrent of uncertainty. Neither of these women wanted to believe that their colleague and friend was involved. Just like I didn't want to believe my client was involved.

Except circumstantial evidence was mounting that she was.

And my disclosure of her name to the detective directly led to her detainment, if not arrest.

But what could law enforcement do with a woman with the level of supernatural power that I believed Isabel had? She was also our only lead. Despite my suspicions about her keeping secrets, my gut still told me she wasn't directly responsible and that we required her involvement to find the missing college students.

I needed to fix this. First course of business: springing Isabel from the slammer.

CHAPTER FIFTEEN

"What do you mean, I can't see her?" I asked in frustration. The polite but firm rebuff from the uniformed officer came immediately.

Dan and I had arrived at the multi-story tan building on Travis Street, sprinting up the outside stairs to rescue our client. Only to hit a roadblock.

"Please let me finish, ma'am."

"My apologies. Please continue," I said, abashed. In my hurry to see my client, I'd interrupted the young man.

"I said, you can't see her… but that's in part because we don't have anybody here by that name."

I furrowed my brow. "You mean she wasn't arrested?"

"That's not my department," he replied. "You'll need to speak with an arresting officer or the detective overseeing her case."

"I'll need to speak with…" My repetition of the words he'd spoken trailed off, and I metaphorically smacked myself on the forehead. "Thank you very much, officer. That's what we'll do." I offered a wide smile, which the correctional officer mirrored, before I spun on my heels and exited the building.

Back in the car, Dan spoke as I withdrew my cellphone from my backpack. "Calling Detective Snyder?"

"Good morning, Detective," I sang out when he answered my call.

"Let me guess why you're calling," he said.

"I'd like to see Isabel."

"When did you become her lawyer?"

"Cheeky."

"That's the only way you're seeing her."

"Did you arrest her?"

A small sigh sounded in my ear. "We brought her in for questioning."

"Because I gave you her name," I pointed out.

"Because she is a person of interest," he snapped back.

"Fair enough," I said, wracking my brain for a way to get in.

"It's not going to happen."

"Are you reading my mind?" I teased, not giving up yet.

"I've already warned the front desk that you might show up."

"So untrusting," I joked, though recognizing that I might need another approach.

"Let us do our jobs," he pleaded. "Surely there's something else you can investigate while we speak to her."

I opened my mouth to object. "You're right," I told him instead, no doubt surprising all of us. "Thank you very much." I heard a spluttered, *you're welcome,* as I ended the call, but mind was already on the realization I'd just had. My eyes met Dan's questioning ones.

"What's up?" he asked.

"The detective is right. We have another area to investigate. I can't believe I missed it."

"Back to the hotel?"

Dan fired up the car and I exchanged a flurry of texts with Mandie during the drive back to the hotel.

"What do you have Mandie working on?" Dan asked after we exited the vehicle in the hotel parking lot.

"Wait until we're inside," I said, checking over my shoulder as we approached the hotel doors. We entered and I waved hello to the desk clerk. Once we crossed the lobby and had convened in our usual spots in the dining area, I withdrew my laptop from my backpack and explained. "We dismissed the sketch artist's bird image too soon."

"The one that Kimberly Roberts had described?"

"Yes." My fingers skimmed over the surface of my keyboard to navigate to my emails. "She's quick."

"Mandie?"

I stilled my fingers and focused on Dan. "First the confusing news."

"Lay it on me."

"Mandie says that there might have been unseasonal fog on the other two nights when the first college students were taken."

"Might have?" he asked.

"There's mention of it on those nights."

"That's good, right?"

"There's mention of it periodically at other times, too. It's not super-rare."

Dan frowned. "So we make a note of it and see if anything else pops to tie it together?"

"Agreed." I fixed him with a determined look. "Back to the bird image. Let's Socratic-method this."

He grinned.

"Why did Isabel hire us?" I began.

"Isabel hired us because of rumors that a Lechuza was kidnapping college students."

"Why did we give that credence?"

"Because you sensed ridiculously high levels of supernatural energy when you met her."

"Why then were we surprised when evidence mounted that Isabel might be a Lechuza?"

Dan frowned as he thought. "Two reasons, I suppose. The first reason we've talked about a number of times, without a clear answer: why would she hire us to find her out, if she's guilty? The second: the image that Kimberly described to the sketch artist was a turkey, not an owl. And an owl is one of the forms a Lechuza takes."

"What does that suggest?"

"That Isabel being a Lechuza isn't related to the kidnappings. And that the turkey might actually be meaningful."

"I'd be careful to state so conclusively that Isabel being a Lechuza isn't related to the kidnappings," I cautioned. "It would still be a mighty big coincidence that she has no bearing on the case. My guess is that whatever she's withholding from us would answer that question."

"Noted."

"But the second point is spot on."

"That the turkey is meaningful?"

"Yep. We were quick to dismiss it, thinking that either Kimberly imagined it, misremembered the appearance, or there was a miscommunication with the police sketch artist."

"That's where we were wrong?"

"I believe so. Earlier, I recalled from my studies several mythological representations of turkeys—but in Native American cultures rather than in Latin American."

"Unlike the Lechuza?"

"Exactly. As opposed to the more recent Mexican folklore regarding the Lechuza, what I recall are Aztec and Hopi gods. The former was known as a jade turkey that represented plagues and the latter had more to do with the rites of spring. Neither seemed relevant to missing college students."

"Unless the Aztec god thinks college students are a plague?" Dan joked.

"Seems unlikely," I said drolly.

"What made you think to revisit the image?"

"The fact that the turkey was white." My doctorate in mythology had been helpful throughout my unusual career, but there was always more to learn. I spun my computer around so Dan could see the email Mandie sent. "It hit me that the color must be significant, and that was something I couldn't recall from my studies."

Dan's eyes moved back and forth as he read Mandie's summary email. She had reverse-searched the turkey image and found I'd almost been on the right track. The white turkey was a little-known representation of an Aztec god, just not the one I'd remembered.

"'The Aztec god Tezcatlipoca usually appears as a jaguar, but sometimes, specifically as the trickster god—I know it's crazy—he appears as a white turkey'," Dan read the email verbatim. "Not another god," he grumbled when he finished.

I chuckled. "That still begs the question. What would an Aztec god want with a bunch of college students?"

Although my question was rhetorical, Dan would not have had a chance to answer, anyway. A forceful wave of supernatural energy rolled over me. I searched out the source of the sudden anxiety, guilt, and sadness battering my internal barrier. My eyes widened.

"Speak of the devil," I muttered. "Or more accurately, the Lechuza." I lifted my chin toward the lobby doors, while I double- and triple-checked the fortification of my stone protection wall to confirm zero gaps.

Dan twisted in his seat. "I guess she wasn't arrested."

I agreed—"I guess not."—moments before Isabel reached our table.

CHAPTER SIXTEEN

Isabel loomed over us for a moment. "May I sit?"

That broke the spell. "Of course," I told her, overcoming my shock at the strength of her supernatural energy, even with my protection wall. I didn't think her power was strong enough to break the barrier, so I wasn't at a huge risk of my physical and emotional experiences becoming confused with hers. But if I maintained this heightened level of protection for very long, I'd crash from exhaustion.

She pulled out the chair closest to me, collapsing into it. "I got your messages, but I thought it would be easier to speak with you in person," she said.

"How did you know we'd be here?" I asked with genuine curiosity.

She shrugged. "It seemed the most logical place to start since it's quiet and you'd have full access to whatever's in your room."

"Rooms," Dan corrected and Isabel arched an eyebrow.

"Not what I meant," she commented blandly.

My face flushed at Dan's interpretation of her comment. At least the exchange broke the inexplicable tension that had risen when she arrived. "You weren't arrested," I stated, rather than asked, since it seemed self-evident.

"I wasn't," she confirmed. "Detective Snyder brought me in for questioning and that was it. Because I'm innocent," she stressed.

"I believe you," I said.

"You do?"

"Yes. Look, do I believe you're withholding information from me?" I asked.

She broke eye contact but did not respond.

"I do believe that. But," I continued, "I don't believe you are directly involved in the disappearance of the college students."

Isabel sagged against the back of the chair in relief. "Thank goodness. You don't know how much it means for you to say that." The anxiety in her surging emotions receded a bit with her statement, also giving me a bit of respite.

"You're welcome. Don't overlook the first part of what I said about you withholding information from us," I warned her.

Her cheeks flamed red. "I won't."

That she did not deny my assumption, and that her guilt flared brighter against my internal barrier, told me I was right. Since she continued to not be forthcoming, I tried to ease into that information. "Why did the detective say he brought you in for questioning?"

"He saw video footage of me talking to Kimberly on the street when she was out for a jog."

"That's it?"

She stared impassively at me. "What else would there be?"

"If I knew, I wouldn't be asking. Did you see the fog that night?" I asked instead.

She continued to stare at me in silence. Zero emotional reaction.

"Isabel? The fog?" I pushed.

"I didn't see any fog," she answered, and the confusion in her tone made me question the relevancy to the case.

"Have you seen unexplained fog before?" I tried another angle.

"I don't understand the question," she said. "I've seen fog. I don't know what unexplained fog even is, so I don't know how to answer that."

Her confusion pinged as genuine. Maybe the fog was an irrelevant anomaly after all.

"How did you know where Kimberly was?" Dan blurted out into the extended silence, and my mouth almost dropped open that we hadn't considered that before.

"That was a question the detective asked, too," I realized.

"This stays between us?" she asked.

A laugh bubbled out before I could stop it. "Look, I'll try, but I can't promise that."

Isabel nodded. "I have a friend who can find people. I didn't ask her how, but she gave me Kimberly's home address."

"Kimberly wasn't staying at her home," Dan interjected.

She nodded again. "My friend also gave me the addresses of her parents and a couple of her best friends."

For a half-second, I considered pursuing the line of questioning about Isabel's possibly shady friend. Then I concluded what the detective probably did: it didn't matter how she got the information since I didn't believe she'd kidnapped any of the students. "Why were you so desperate to locate Kimberly?" I asked instead.

Isabel's leg bounced in her seat and a curious mix of desperation and worry swirled in my mind.

With difficulty, I compartmentalized the emotions. "Isabel?"

She opened and closed her mouth. Her reticence had to be related to the information she was withholding.

"What did you talk to Kimberly about?" I moved on to, hopefully, an easier question for her to answer.

"I asked her what she saw that night outside the bar."

"And?"

"She just repeated that she saw a bird."

"A white bird."

"Yes, a white bird," Isabel said, her voice betraying a hint of irritation.

"That's it?" I asked, incredulous. "The conversation looked like it lasted longer than three or four sentences."

"I told you, I asked her what she saw outside the bar that night," Isabel insisted.

I suspected she was playing a game of semantics. "What precisely did you ask her?"

"I asked her who she saw that night."

"Who? Not what?"

Isabel crossed her arms over her chest.

"Do you know who kidnapped the college students?"

Her arms dropped to dangle at her sides and her brown eyes filled with tears. "I might," she admitted.

CHAPTER SEVENTEEN

"Isabel, we can't help you if you aren't straight with us," I implored her. "Please tell us what you know."

"Bear with me," she began, "I need to start at the beginning."

I nodded as I angled in my chair to give Isabel all of my attention. Dan reopened his computer tablet to take notes.

"My brother and I were the first generation born in the United States. Our parents had crossed over the border from Mexico into El Paso."

I noted her Mexican accent thickened as she relayed her history.

"We had a standard childhood, as far as I know." She shrugged. "We didn't go hungry. Our parents always kept a roof over our heads. Gave us a stable life."

"That's great," I said into her pregnant pause, assuming the story was about to turn based on my team's prior knowledge of her time in foster care.

"Then," she said and swallowed audibly. "One winter when my brother and I were in high school, an electric heating blanket in the living room caught fire. To this day, I don't know if someone left it on, or it just malfunctioned. But that blanket burned the house down. My brother and I were very heavy sleepers." Her breath hitched and I steeled myself against the onslaught of her misery. "I remember my father coming into our room to wake us. I remember the smell of the smoke, the acrid burning in the back of my throat, even the sound of the crackling fire. And I remember that after he got us out, our mom wasn't with us, so he ran back in to get her. Juan and I never saw them again." She wept silently, tears running in rivers down her face.

I blinked back my own tears that threatened. "I'm so sorry, Isabel," I offered, despite knowing that would be insufficient for such a traumatic loss.

She wrapped her arms around her chest to self-soothe for a moment, then wiped the tears from her cheeks with her fingers. "Thank you."

Dan and I waited for her to compose herself.

"After that, we went into the foster care system. All our relatives were in Mexico. We had no one here except each other."

"That must have been comforting, to have each other."

"It was," she agreed before her expression hardened. "The foster system was not good for us."

"What happened?" I asked in a soft tone.

"We were teenage siblings. For the years until we aged out of the system, we bounced between homes where the foster parents only wanted us for the paycheck and our presumed self-sufficiency. Which we had to develop, given the neglect," she finished bitterly.

"I'm sorry that was your experience," I said, sad that so many children in the foster care system didn't receive the love they needed. I'd worked with children in the system when I was training for my counseling graduate degree. While many homes were stellar, not all of them should have taken in children.

"It was worse for Juan. He started stuttering."

"He developed a stutter after entering foster care?"

She nodded. "He was also just an awkward teenager. Because of the stutter and his awkwardness, he was a magnet for bullies."

My heart hurt for the young teenagers surviving one trauma after another.

She bit her lower lip.

I suspected we were about to get into the consequences of all this trauma.

"It was around this time that I discovered the Wiccan religion." She half-smiled. "I loved the beauty of the connection to the Earth, and the idea that intention can shape reality. For about a year, I researched the details and just really dug into it. All the while, the bullying became relentless with Juan." She placed her palms flat on the table. "I've never told this story to anyone."

"Please trust us," I coaxed her.

"One day, I was engaging in my daily practice. Sort of like a meditation on my connection to the Goddess. I became overwhelmed with anger toward the bullies, anxiety for my brother, and helplessness from not being able to do more. I begged the Goddess to help me." Isabel paused in her explanation to stare at her hands, which had remained unmoving. "Since the fire, I'd noticed small differences in how I moved through the world. It's hard to explain. It wasn't like I could shoot fireballs from my fingertips or anything."

I matched her lop-sided grin at the small joke.

"My Wiccan practice helped me feel the energy flowing through me. That day when I begged the Goddess for help, everything changed."

"What happened?"

"I'm not 100 percent certain," she acknowledged. "There was…not a voice exactly…more like a *knowing* that I could tap into this new power and have a way to protect my brother. I didn't realize what I'd accepted until later that week. My brother came home from school and I heard him crying in the bathroom. He didn't want to tell me what had happened, but eventually he gave me the name of a boy who had been merciless."

Her gaze swung from mine to Dan's before finding mine again.

"A few nights later, I went to a park where I'd learned that boy liked to hang out and smoke cigarettes. I didn't have a plan. Just a feeling. When I got there, and saw him leaning against a bike rack with a couple of his friends, I allowed the anger and righteousness to swell within me." She lifted her hand to her mouth as if to bite her nails and then dropped the hand back to the tabletop.

"Tell us what happened," I encouraged.

She swallowed audibly again. "My bones began to ache, then shift. My arms extended to become white wings. Every sound in the park amplified in my ears. I changed. When I looked down, I was shocked to see that I'd shifted into a human-sized bird. Later, when I researched, it confirmed what I suspected. I'd become an owl, the animal form of Lechuza."

"That's incredible," I breathed, wanting to say something to acknowledge such a powerful transformation.

"To be clear," she added in a sardonic tone, "unlike what it says online, I did not sell my soul to the devil."

The three of us chuckled, breaking the rising tension.

"Then what happened?" I asked.

"Then I could protect my brother," she said proudly. "Word spread very fast that if anybody messed with Juan, La Lucheza would visit them. And since the rumors said she often appeared before people died, the subtle threat was that she might kill people." She held her hands in a prayer-like position in front of her chest. "Let me emphasize, though, that I *never* killed anyone. Just scared them."

"That's why you hired me. Kimberly reported she saw a human-sized bird and then rumors spread that a Lechuza was behind the disappearances."

She nodded. "I knew I didn't do it, and I couldn't imagine there was another Lechuza in town." Now she gave a one-shoulder shrug. "But I couldn't be certain. When I was researching online for options, and saw in Dan's blog that you'd be in Dallas... well, that seemed like the Goddess providing."

A lot had crystallized with Isabel's story. Except for one thing. "Your story is extraordinary, and I still believe you that you aren't directly involved in the college student disappearances," I assured her. "What I don't understand is how you now think you know who has kidnapped them?"

Her voice dropped to a whisper. "I think my brother kidnapped them."

CHAPTER EIGHTEEN

Absolute silence followed her bombshell statement. I recovered my voice first. "What makes you think it's your brother?" I asked, choosing that over the many other questions fighting to be asked.

Instead of a verbal answer, she withdrew her phone from her purse and, a few clicks later, handed it to me.

I gasped and showed the internet page to Dan, who also startled at what he saw. Two images dominated the page. The first image was a photograph of a wooden signpost welcoming visitors to the *Kingdom of Tezcatlipoca*. The second image was a graphic of a flag with thick black and turquoise stripes. But what had elicited my gasp was the stylized white turkey in the middle of the flag.

"What is this?" I asked, baffled by what I was seeing.

"Are you familiar with micronations?" she asked in response.

I exchanged a glance with Dan before answering. "I'm familiar with them in a general sense. Is this a micronation?" I peered closer at the website. "Is this your brother's micronation?"

Isabel nodded and clicked on the website's menu before handing the phone back to me. The *About* page showed an unsmiling man, half-hidden in shadow, wearing jeans and a black shirt, with his arms crossed, almost daring the viewer to challenge him.

The man's face was more obscured than not, yet something about him seemed familiar. I studied what I could see of his face and stance, frustrated that I was unable to place him. Then I read the description and my frustration turned to bewilderment.

"Who is John Castor?" I asked in confusion after reading that name as the supreme leader of the Kingdom of Tezcatlipoca.

"That's my brother."

"I thought your brother's name was Juan Garcia. Is there a second brother?" I asked in continued confusion.

"He changed his name after he left El Paso," she explained.

John had provided a thorough narrative on his website. There would be a lot for Mandie to research. I read aloud about the unusual history of the Kingdom of Tezcatlipoca.

John Castor struggled to find his place in the world until the Aztec god Tezcatlipoca brought him to the rolling plains of north Texas. Here, John established the Kingdom of Tezcatlipoca, to welcome all who similarly struggled and to protect them from the harshness of the world. With the Aztec god as inspiration, John developed the kingdom's flag. He also designed and built a home to serve both as the political seat of the kingdom and as a place for followers to stay until they constructed their own similar abode. All were welcome and would live, work, and serve together for the betterment of the whole. Scrolling to the bottom of the page, I saw an image of a sprawling single-story ranch house, pushing 4000 square feet, if I had to guess.

"It's… interesting," I said, in as delicate a way as I could. "And I can follow how the white turkey in the flag suggested a circumstantial connection to your brother. But how do you make the leap from a white turkey on your brother's micronation flag to the belief that he's kidnapping college students?"

Her cheeks colored. "I didn't suspect him at first," she allowed. "The first college student disappearance didn't register with me, to be honest. I hoped the woman just needed a break from her studies."

A surge of guilt rose in me that I identified as coming from Isabel. My bubble visualization isolated the emotion and then released it to float far above and away from my wall of protection.

"When the second college student disappeared so soon after the first—" she said, her voice cutting off with a sharp inhalation. "That caught my attention more."

"That's understandable," I sympathized. "The second disappearance so soon after the first made a lot more people sit up and take notice."

"When the third college student described her attempted kidnapping, I had a terrible feeling." She stared at me, the desperation in her eyes and her energy begging me—no, imploring me—to believe her and understand.

"That's when you came to hire me," I finished.

She nodded. "When Kimberly told the police that a bird tried to kidnap her. Well. The rumors of a Lechuza ran rampant."

"And with your, um, intimate knowledge of Lechuza," I sidestepped a direct comment, "you knew that wasn't likely to be the case."

Dan interjected, lifting his stylus from his computer tablet where he'd been taking notes, "I'm still not understanding how that led to your brother as the suspect in your mind."

"When you showed me the police sketch artist's drawing, I knew," she answered, as the connection slammed home to me.

"That's when you saw that Kimberly described a turkey, not an owl. The rumors had it wrong."

"Not just a turkey," she clarified. "A white turkey."

"Stronger, but still just circumstantial," I mused. The guilt poured off of Isabel. I gasped at the onslaught as she continued speaking, unaware of the impact she was having on me.

"I called my brother."

"When?" I asked, my voice shaking. I felt Dan's eyes on me.

"Right after you showed me the image," she whispered, staring at her lap. Her bouncing leg shook the table.

"Kimberly disappeared right after that," Dan stated.

Isabel raised tear-filled eyes to implore us. "I don't want to believe it's him, but how else do you explain this? A man-sized bird attempted to kidnap a woman, and when I call my brother to ask him about it, she disappears without a trace?"

"I have a question about that," Dan said. "Kimberly said a man-sized bird tried to kidnap her. Not," he stressed, "a man dressed as a bird."

I suspected where Dan was going with this, but Isabel's expression of confusion suggested she did not.

"Please tell us your brother isn't actually shapeshifting and channeling the Aztec god," Dan concluded.

Isabel gave him a bemused look. "Of course not. I can't explain why Kimberly was so convinced it was an actual man-sized bird versus a man dressed in a costume. But I think I understand what Juan, I mean John, is trying to do."

"What?" I asked.

"John wants to emulate the trickster god."

"In what way?"

"By building up followers for his micronation to become their supreme leader. After years of being bullied, he wants to be adored."

"How would they join? There doesn't seem to be a way to contact John," I commented after scanning the page for an email or contact form.

"There isn't," Isabel confirmed.

"Then how are you in contact with him?" Dan asked the obvious question.

"Something changed by the time I graduated high school," she answered with a seeming non sequitur. "He became increasingly distant. We lost contact after leaving El Paso. I didn't, and still don't, understand what happened." She sniffled. "I miss him." A wave of sadness tinged with guilt lapped against my internal protective wall.

"That had to be tough," I empathized, wondering if the guilt was from her perceived failure to maintain contact, and figured she was working her way toward answering Dan's question.

"I kept the same phone number all these years just in case he'd want to reach out," she continued.

"He finally did?" I guessed.

She nodded. "Six months ago." Her voice dropped, even though there were no other patrons within hearing distance. "He called me out of the blue. I was thrilled. Until he told me why. He said he knew I had become a Lechuza during high school."

"You didn't think he knew?" I asked.

"Not at all," she answered. "I don't know how he knew. He didn't even really focus on that in the conversation, except to say that, because of what I was, I should understand why he would want to emulate a powerful being."

"I'm guessing he didn't appreciate your lack of understanding," I theorized.

"No. He asked me to join him in his micronation." She shook her head as if still in disbelief. "I had to look up what a micronation was because when he first asked me to join the Kingdom of Tezcatlipoca, I honestly thought it was a cult."

"I mean, to be fair, it sounds like a cult," Dan added.

"Micronations in the current era are kind of entertaining when they really exist," Isabel insisted.

"Wait, do some not really exist?" I asked in confusion.

Isabel chuckled at my question before sobering. "I did a ton of research after I spoke with John. Which is also when I learned he had unofficially changed his name from Juan Garcia to John Castor," she added in an offhand manner.

"Did he say why?" I asked, curious and not sure if it would be relevant.

"He said he needed a break from the scared, bullied kid of his youth," she told us.

"That makes sense," I replied.

"What did you learn from your research?" Dan asked.

"Micronations have existed for quite a while. Their levels of development vary. Some have an established governmental setup similar to the US. Those might have legislative, judicial, and executive branches and ministers of various departments. They can have a fair number of members who live together on a plot of land, most often in a rural area. Other micronations are basically in name only. They may be based in someone's house in the middle of nowhere, even have a charter, but they have only one person, and that person does it for fun. At any given time, the state of Texas has a dozen or so active micronations. As you might imagine, especially where it's just a single individual, they go inactive when that person moves on, passes away, or just loses interest."

"Wow," Dan commented. "I had no idea."

"That's what your brother tried to create with the Kingdom of Tezcatlipoca," I summarized.

"He was so proud of himself," she said, almost wistfully. "I wished I could have said yes."

"You declined," I concluded.

"Of course I did," she said with a sigh. "I'm not giving up my life to live in the middle of Wilbarger County, Texas while my brother plays god."

"What did he say when you told him no?" I asked.

"He said I would regret it."

CHAPTER NINETEEN

"He threatened you?" I asked this question in a sharp voice.

"No, no, no," Isabel hurried to answer. "Or at least, I assumed he meant that I would regret it by missing out on the wonder of communing together for Tezcatlipoca."

"And now?" I probed.

"Now I'm not so sure what he meant," she admitted.

"You believe he's kidnapping them because they won't join on their own?" I speculated. "That seems like a bit of a leap."

"I know," she said. "But how else can you explain Kimberly's disappearance after I called him?"

"I can't," I answered honestly. "Let's walk through how this could be playing out." The focus on order helped me manage Isabel's continued onslaught of distressed emotions.

"I think he tried to get legitimate followers," Isabel said. "I've been stalking his page for months and he hasn't added new members." She clicked a few times, then showed us the sadly empty membership listing on John's micronation website.

"He might not be updating the website," I offered as an alternative explanation.

"Even though Kimberly reported a man-sized white bird tried to grab her? That she described to the sketch artist as a turkey?" Isabel asked with a single eyebrow raised.

"I don't disagree that it's suggestive or circumstantial, but it's not directly incriminating," I stated.

"Even though his stated goal is to gain new followers? And he asked me to join him? And there's a white turkey on the flag of his micronation named after an Aztec God?" She ticked off the questions on her fingers as her voice rose.

"How do we think John might first seek a new follower?" I asked Isabel and Dan, trying to redirect her energy. "Do we believe he's approaching people prior to actually kidnapping them, since there's no way to contact him through the website?" I pointed at Isabel. "Like he did for you."

"I would think yes," she answered slowly. "Give them a chance to join on their own."

"When they refuse, like you did," Dan picked up the thread, "he forces them to."

"Although he didn't force me," Isabel pointed out.

We sat with that inconsistency for a moment.

"Maybe because he didn't believe you would say anything to anyone else," Dan theorized.

"Given what it took for you to disclose to us—" She flushed at my statement. "—he seems to have been mostly right about that," I said.

"It's also been months since he asked me," she reminded us before agreeing, "I'm probably an anomaly."

"Maybe he regrouped after your refusal. Took time to consider other options," I mused.

"Gave himself time to plan his new approach?" Dan asked.

"Most likely," I agreed. "Eliminating you, Isabel, from consideration, we're left with several questions. How fast would this process happen? Would he give them time to think about the offer? Or would that be too risky? That if they say no, he risks them mentioning him to someone else? I'd guess that it happens the same day so it minimizes risk of discovery," I answered myself.

Isabel nodded. "I agree."

"I wouldn't think he would hurt you for refusing, since he didn't kidnap you. Do you think he would hurt the college students? What's his game plan? How is he planning to keep them in his kingdom?" I asked my questions almost stream of consciousness, before pausing to let Isabel answer.

Dan jumped in first. "Doc is on point with her questions; assuming John *is* the one kidnapping the students for refusing his offer, is he brainwashing them somehow to stay?"

"He doesn't have that kind of power, does he?" I asked, a feeling of disquiet growing.

Isabel gave me a look similar to when Dan had asked if John was shapeshifting into the form of a bird. "Of course not," she stated.

That sense of disquiet grew stronger. Was that mine or hers? Was she as confident as she sounded about her brother not having supernatural powers?

"Did you tell any of this to Detective Snyder when he brought you in for questioning?" I asked instead.

She broke eye contact, which gave me my answer.

"Why not?" I asked.

"I went out to the micronation, pretending I might change my mind," she began.

"That was risky," Dan interrupted, "if you thought he was a kidnapper."

"I needed to see for myself. He believed me and offered me a tour."

"How did that go?" I questioned.

"I drove out to this, honestly, beautiful home. That he built himself," she added, clearly proud of at least that part of her brother's accomplishment. "It's quite gorgeous." She nodded, almost to herself, as she refocused on the point of her story. "The area is remote. It's the typical north Texas open grassland dotted with scattered mesquite savannas." Now she rolled her eyes. "He said Tezcatlipoca led him there to allow the God's sunlight to bathe his followers."

That statement sounded like the type of religious delusion the clients I had seen while earning my counseling psychology degree would say. Religious delusions that were often associated with schizophrenia or bipolar disorder. And John was statistically the right age for the former. "Is there any chance he may have had a psychotic break?" I asked carefully.

"I can't rule it out, but I don't think so," Isabel answered. "He has an unusual belief system," she admitted, "but it seems like more of a defense mechanism than a psychotic break."

I smiled at the psychology jargon, which could be typical of me, given my background, but was less common with clients.

"Yes, I took quite a few psychology classes in school," she replied in response to my mirthful expression.

"What did you see during the tour?" I asked, directing her back to the story.

"Nothing suspicious," she offered in summary before expounding. "The house was lovely but empty. I only saw one vehicle, an SUV. There were no other buildings on the grounds. I believe he said he has over twenty acres."

"How did he buy that property and afford to build the house?" It occurred to me that if he began within a few years of high school, he could have been in his early twenties when he started developing his micronation. The middle of nowhere in north Texas might not be too expensive, but it wasn't free.

Isabel frowned. "I don't know. He didn't say, and I didn't think to ask."

I shot a glance at Dan and he made a note, probably to ask Mandie to research property deeds in the area as a start.

"Why didn't you tell the police about this?" I asked my question again.

"I didn't see anything that suggested people were being held there," she answered, just a touch defensively. "I was—am—afraid of what might happen if I tell the police. What if the police hurt him? What if he hurts the missing women?"

"If he even has the missing women," I commented.

"I still don't know what to do," she said.

I didn't need my clairempathy to know that fear, worry, and guilt were all at war within Isabel as she tried to choose the right path forward. In theory, the logical course of action was to share this information with the police. However, that could be considered a colossal waste of their time if Isabel saw nothing suspicious out at the micronation.

A brilliant, only slightly ridiculous, plan popped into my head.

"I have an idea," I said.

CHAPTER TWENTY

"I want to go on record as stating this is a terrible idea," Dan groused at me as we sat at the bar in The Broken Tap.

"I believe you've already gone on the record with that statement," I reminded him. When we'd entered the space, I'd considered sitting at the long, high-top tables opposite the bar, but decided that wasn't conducive to attracting a kidnapper. We came early since we'd heard the bar was popular in Wichita Falls, and we were glad we did. The place was loud with enthusiastic patron chatter. Tall ceilings coupled with brick walls to manage the echo. Before entering, I'd shorn up my wall of protection, but thus far, that didn't seem necessary. Although there was a wide range of physical and emotional experiences happening in the bar, none of it was overly strong, nor did anything strike me as supernatural.

"This is a terrible idea," he repeated. "Getting yourself kidnapped? How do you know this will even work?"

"I don't," I acknowledged. His concern was cute, but I was counting in part on my clairempathy to keep me ahead of our alleged kidnapper. "Remember, all three women went to a bar before they disappeared."

"Yes, but they're college students," he said, sounding exasperated and worried. "They go to bars. It's not necessarily connected. Besides, boss, you're not a college student."

"Thanks, dude," I retorted. "I'm small and look young for my age. I might be able to fake it enough for him to be interested." From a distance, at least, I thought I could pass for a college student. I was only in my early thirties, and describing myself as small wasn't an exaggeration: only 5'2" and 100 pounds soaking wet. I'd pulled my long auburn hair into a high ponytail, worn no makeup, and added the concert t-shirt plus tighter-than-normal-for-me jeans I'd found at a quick stop at a resale shop in town.

Dan scanned the bar's interior. "I don't see anybody who looks like that shaded picture of John on his website or how Isabel described her brother."

He wasn't wrong. And, unfortunately, we didn't have additional information on John Castor né Juan Garcia. Dan had chatted with Mandie while I tried on clothing. She'd confirmed that her internet forager had thus far proven unsuccessful at finding information under either name, other than what we already knew. It definitely suggested that Juan had become John and done his best to stay off the grid.

"I doubt he's here yet. Time for Stage Two," I enthused.

"Why are you so excited to be kidnapped?" Dan grumbled. "Besides, when did we break this into stages?"

"Anyway," I responded, ignoring his rhetorical questions, "time for you to leave."

At my instruction, Dan remained still. He didn't retrieve his phone, nor did he say anything.

"Dan?"

"I'm not comfortable with this plan," he said in a quiet voice.

His heightened worry and fear pinged off my internal barrier, surprising me. Not because he was concerned, but because his laid-back nature meant that my barrier rarely needed to block him. "You won't be far," I reminded him.

"I know, but…" he trailed off.

"Do you trust me?"

"You know I do."

"Then trust that our plan will work."

Without another word, Dan pulled his phone out of his backpack and called Mandie. We'd thought about having him pretend to receive a phone call but wanted his end of the conversation to sound authentic.

I heard Mandie's tinny voice on the other end of the call as the two of them exchanged pleasantries before she made her request for his assistance. We'd joked earlier about what that something should be and finally went with realistic. She was asking him to watch her kids while she picked up her husband whose car was still in the shop. This worked for many reasons, not the least of which was the fact that Mandie and her husband had four children under the age of thirteen.

Dan promised he'd be there soon and ended the call. I waited expectantly.

"I'm so sorry, Sarah, but Mandie needs me to watch the kids. Do you mind if I duck out? We'll catch up another time?" Dan deserved an acting award for the disappointed look on his face matching his downbeat tone.

"Of course," I assured him, resting my hand on his forearm. "You're a great friend to help out like that."

He offered a blinding smile in thanks, which I mirrored. Then he stood from the stool. I hopped down from mine, losing my step and falling into him. He caught me and there was an awkward, heated moment—I reminded myself that he was my employee and ten years younger—before we separated.

Dan recovered faster, offering a quick wave, and then jetting for the exit. I spun on my heels to choose where to go next.

There. Perfect.

A group of four women surrounded a pool table at the back. They appeared to be early twenties, so hopefully, college students. The women paused in their play as I reached their group.

I waved. "Hi, my friend just ditched me to be responsible. Do you mind if I join you?" I asked in a bright voice.

The woman closest to me, a brunette with hazel eyes and a teal shirt that said *Hotter 'n Hell Hundred*, held out her hand, which I shook. "Of course. I'm Meg. Nice to meet you. The more the merrier."

"Thanks. I'm just visiting a friend—"

"The friend who ditched you?" another brunette at the pool table teased.

"Yeah." I laughed with faux self-consciousness and, pointing at the shirt, resumed my question. "What's the Hotter 'n Hell Hundred?"

Meg's face lit up. "I'm a volunteer most years, though I have been known to actually ride." She regaled me with stories about people choosing to ride bicycles for up to 100 miles in the blistering Texas heat in August, hence the name.

My attempt to break the ice successful, we settled into companionable chatter. I periodically removed and replaced a stone in my wall of protection. Nothing. Nothing supernatural or even outside the ordinary for a crowd. After another hour passed, I wanted to make something happen.

Dropping my voice to just above a whisper, I asked the four women, "Have you heard about the missing college students?"

All four solemnly nodded their heads. Meg spoke first. "It's freaky, knowing that fellow college students can just—

poof—disappear." She snapped her fingers on the word *poof.*

"Do you all go to Midwestern State University?" I asked.

Four heads nodded again.

"I heard about it from my friend, but he said nobody knows anything. Have any of you heard anything about what's happened?"

They exchanged glances, but there was nothing in them to suggest they possessed any big news or secret knowledge.

"This will sound crazy," Meg said, her voice pitched low to match mine. "Have you heard of Lechuza?"

I shook my head in the negative.

"It's a Mexican folktale of sorts in Texas. There are different versions. In most of them, a woman, often a witch, makes a deal with the devil to seek revenge on men who hurt women. She is said to appear before people die. She's also said to take babies."

"Eww," the other brunette interjected.

Meg ignored the interruption and focused on telling me the story. "The rumor is that it's a Lechuza making the women disappear."

"That *is* freaky," I agreed, then frowned as if something had just occurred to me. "You said a Lechuza takes revenge on men mostly, or sometimes she grabs babies. What does that have to do with college women?"

The women stopped moving around the pool table as they considered my question.

Meg shrugged. "I'm not certain, except that we heard one of the missing women wasn't taken immediately."

"What do you mean?" I asked.

"She said that a giant bird tried to grab her," Meg said. "Right outside this bar."

All four women turned to stare at the front door. I had to admit it was a bit freaky, and a tendril of anxiety moved up my spine.

I laughed and the women rewarded me with smiles, tension dissipating, at least for now.

"It sounds bonkers," Meg continued. "But that's what she said. And since a Lechuza appears as a human-sized owl, it makes sense as a theory."

After that confirmation of the Lechuza rumors, the ladies had nothing else related to the case to share. The night wore on and I never felt even a sliver of supernatural energy, nor did I see anyone who fit John's description.

When it passed midnight, I decided it was time for Stage Three. I suppressed a chuckle at what Dan's commentary would be on my internal declaration. I forced a wide yawn and pointedly checked the time on my cellphone.

"Are you fixin' to leave?" the quietest of the four women piped up to ask.

With a vague gesture toward the door, I answered in the affirmative and attempted to make my goodbyes.

"How are you getting home?" Meg asked.

I couldn't very well tell them that Dan was outside in the rental waiting for me if needed when I left. "I'll call a rideshare."

The women appeared uneasy.

"Do you want one of us to wait with you outside?" Meg asked. "Especially given what we told you about the college student disappearances."

"That's not necessary," I assured her as a clever ruse occurred to me. "I'll request it in here and I'll head out when it's arriving." I pointed toward the pool table. "No reason for you to disrupt your game. I'll be perfectly safe walking five feet from one door to another."

Meg looked like she wanted to argue, but said nothing when I pulled my phone out to request the rideshare. I was glad that my privacy screen kept her from seeing that I was faking. After completing the steps in my head while I moved my fingers, and hoping that looked legitimate enough, I glanced up from my phone.

"I'll let you know when it's here," I promised them.

"If you're sure," Meg said, her fisted hand radiating tension on her hip.

"Yes, I'm sure," I responded. About five minutes later, I waved the phone at them. "I'm heading out. It was so nice to meet all of you." When it looked like Meg might try to follow me anyway, in another fit of cleverness, I called the waitress over and handed her several bills. "A round of drinks for my new friends." I turned to them. "Thanks y'all for showing me some great Texas hospitality."

Then I snuck toward the front door while the waitress distracted the women. I slowed my steady stride as I neared the door. Instead, I wobbled a bit, slurring apologies when I bumped into a few patrons.

I paused at the threshold for a moment, unsure of my plan, since I still didn't feel anything supernatural. However, the plan centered on John kidnapping me. My pulse jumped at the thought. I deepened my shallow breaths, then clenched and unclenched my fists at my sides, trying to shake off the apprehension. Knowing that Dan was parked up the street at the corner spurred me forward. This either worked, or Dan would drive us back to the hotel, the plan a bust.

I stepped out into the balmy spring night.

CHAPTER TWENTY-ONE

At first, nothing changed. I had removed a stone from my wall of protection as I continued my charade of walking tipsily. Still nothing. Disappointment swelled. Then pinpricks of *something* hit my mind.

I halted about ten feet from the front door of the bar and surveyed my surroundings. No pedestrians were present. Just around the corner up the street, I saw the rental and took comfort in knowing Dan was there to intervene if necessary. We planned though to rely on the GPS tracker hidden in my shoe.

The pinpricks increased, a weird sensation in my brain almost like icicles combined with the warmth of promise. A sense of righteousness filled me, and I knew I was on a divine path.

"What the—" I stared in awe.

A wall of dense fog or smoke shimmered at the street corner closest to Dan in the car. The diffuse cloud didn't have an obvious origin. Sniffing the air, it smelled clean. The unusual apparition was fog, not smoke. Like on the security video! Fear surged when I realized that the fog had obscured Dan's rental. The fog rolled closer. My heartbeat jumped erratically in my chest.

And yet, that feeling of righteousness grew.

This was the correct path. I just needed to accept my role.

A figure emerged from the fog.

I dropped my hands to my sides, gaping in disbelief.

Walking toward me was a giant bird. Exactly like the white turkey Kimberly had described. I squinted at the figure, then blinked several times, but the image didn't change. Not a mirage.

My legs felt rooted to the spot. From fear, the fog, or the turkey, I had no idea.

The turkey drew closer. It walked like a human as opposed to strutting like a turkey. My short-circuiting brain couldn't decipher if that had any meaning. It probably did.

My breathing sounded ragged to my ears.

The fog swarmed around me, creating a cocoon. Only the turkey and I existed in the world. Nothing remained visible outside of the cocoon.

When the turkey stopped just outside of arm's reach, my gaze roved over it from top to bottom, trying to make sense of the vision while the pinpricks of icy warmth flayed my protective wall.

Standing about six feet tall, a downy white fuzz covered the turkey's sinewy body. My brain struggled to comprehend the human-male-appearing features of its face surrounded by rough, red skin topped by the bald crown of its head.

The movement of brilliant white feathers where arms would be drew my attention. The turkey extended out its wings in a slow, flaunting style. It had to have a 10-foot wingspan.

The turkey was incredible. Questions swirled as the analytical side of my brain perked up. Was this Tezcatlipoca? Or was this John shifting into Tezcatlipoca's representation in corporeal form? Or something else?

The strange icy, yet warm, pinpricks became an exquisite pain in my mind.

"Stop!" I screamed at the creature. My knees threatened to buckle from the fear, yet my hands stayed fisted against my thighs as anger raged inside.

How dare anyone try to stop me!

I stared into the depthless obsidian eyes of the turkey, my brain begging for quiet release. A tangle of murky brown, dark gray, and intense red swirled around. Just like with Isabel. I had only a second to connect the unusual manifestation of emotions as colors before the flood of emotions overwhelmed my internal stone barrier. It crashed into a pile of rubble in my mind. Vomit burned the back of my throat. My shoulders hunched to prepare to defend myself. Against what? And how?

I was defenseless.

In my last seconds of consciousness, Dan's terrified voice cried out my name.

Darkness consumed me.

CHAPTER TWENTY-TWO

Comfortable warmth enveloped me. I snuggled deeper into the pillowy bed. My nose tickled from the scent of vanilla in the air. I inhaled contentedly.

Then a sense of disquiet rose as my brain realized that this was not home, nor was it a hotel that I recalled—

Someone had kidnapped me!

A moment of satisfaction flared that my plan worked. Then I gripped the no-longer-comfortable bedspread. My plan worked…

Where was I?

I opened my eyes and took stock of my surroundings. At first, I thought it was still nighttime. Shadowy darkness covered most of the room. A sliver of light allowed me to see that I appeared to be in a bedroom. I stretched my arms out and could not reach the edges of the bed. So, probably king-size. A small dresser sat against the wall opposite. No other furniture. No wall hangings. No windows.

Where was the light coming from?

I searched for the origins of the sliver of light. A tiny nightlight was plugged into an outlet next to the door.

The door.

Bolting upright, I threw off the thick comforter and leaped from the bed, thankful that I still wore most of my clothes from the night before. Someone had thoughtfully removed my shoes. A quick scan of the carpeted floor. There. Next to the dresser.

I flew to the door. My heart sank when I saw the door had no interior knob. I brushed my fingers against the blank plate that replaced the knob. The single-sided doorknob effectively locked me in. I placed my hands against the door and pushed anyway. No movement at all.

My teeth chattering despite the warmth in the room caused me to bite my tongue. I swallowed in a reflexive response to the coppery taste of blood in my mouth. A brick in my stomach prevented me from assessing if I was hungry, which might have helped me gauge the passage of time.

Of course, I didn't have my phone. I had no idea where it was. A vague recollection of hearing Dan yell my name surfaced. Did my kidnapper leave my phone behind on the street? If not, maybe Dan could track me. If so, did Dan grab it? I hoped so. I'd want it back when I got out of here.

The emotional lift I got from the thought of leaving plummeted when the next thought was about how to do so.

I didn't know where I was. I didn't know how long I'd been here. I didn't know for certain who had grabbed me.

Pacing back and forth on the carpet, fear crept up and fell back in line with my circling thoughts.

My best guess was that it had been less than 6-8 hours since the kidnapping. It couldn't have been longer. I didn't yet need to use the bathroom. I didn't feel weak from lack of food or water. Nobody rescued me.

What if my kidnapper left me here to die?

That thought triggered a wave of icy dread to wash over me.

Wait.

I shook my head to clear my mind, wondering at my disconnected and discombobulated thoughts.

Dan and I had planned for this.

I raced toward my shoes resting next to the small white dresser. Sitting cross-legged on the light-colored carpet, I picked up the left shoe.

Relief flooded me when I stuck my finger up against the underside of the shoe's tongue and felt the rigid edges of the GPS tracker we'd placed there.

"Thank goodness he didn't find it." I breathed into the stillness, slowing my heartbeat with measured breaths.

It would be okay. I put my shoes on in anticipation of being rescued.

Worry bubbled to the surface that if I was indeed being held at John Castor's Kingdom of Tezcatlipoca micronation, there might not be enough signal strength for the tracker to transmit my location.

No. I couldn't think that way.

Help was on the way.

They had to be… Right?

CHAPTER TWENTY-THREE

The maelstrom in my mind froze. A faint thumping from above clued me into the fact that I most likely was underground. Unless a large animal was on the roof, I thought grimly to myself. If I was indeed underground, that would fit what Isabel had said about seeing no evidence of people on the property or in the house. They weren't *in* the house; they were *under* it.

Thump, thump, thump.

I strained to identify the noise. Even as faint as the sound was to my ears, I surmised the sound was still too loud to be footsteps. And it seemed too steady and rhythmic to be the opening and closing of doors. Could it be a water hammer? That seemed plausible, especially if someone was upstairs running water, like for a shower or bath.

My chest tightened at this sign of another person in the house. Someone in the shower wouldn't be here to rescue me. I tilted my head sideways, lifting my ear, as if that would enable me to hear the sound clearer. It didn't.

After a few minutes, the sound stopped. It hit me that since I could hear the sound from another floor, maybe that meant I could yell out for the college students. If they were here, maybe I could try to communicate with them.

I nixed that plan almost as soon as I had it. The pro of the plan was that if I successfully communicated with the women, I'd have explicit confirmation they were here. Unfortunately, the con of the plan was that if I didn't reach them, I still wouldn't know if they were down here with me because a negative couldn't prove something existed. Worse, it might draw our captor's attention.

Our captor, named Castor. I giggled with rising hysteria at my internal rhyming joke.

I sat on the bed and closed my eyes, resolving to maintain my calm and composure until someone arrived, whether that was help or—

A new sound. More of a softer thud. Then silence.

And then a faint click at the door to my room. Unlocking a key?

My heart in my throat, I swiveled my head like a wild woman. A futile search; like I'd magically find some new implement in the minimally-furnished room to defend myself with.

As the door swung open, I held my breath, frantically reminding myself that if my kidnapper had wanted to harm me, he already could have.

A twenty-something male with a five-o'clock shadow stood in the doorway. He had short curly brown hair and bright blue eyes fringed by long eyelashes. His slight frame and average height threw me for a second. The turkey had appeared at least six feet tall. Uncertainty rose. Could this be someone else?

Something about him pulled at me. Was this John Castor? I wouldn't have bet my life on the man in front of me being the man in the picture on the website. There was something else niggling at the back of my mind.

Belatedly, I noticed the tray he held. My stomach growled at the sight of eggs, toast, and a small plastic glass of something on the tray. Orange juice was my guess since it was breakfast food and I didn't smell coffee.

"Are you hungry?"

The melodic cadence of his voice wormed its way into my brain and I smiled gratefully. "Starving." It shocked me that I was. The brick that had taken up residence in my stomach had dissolved with the appearance of the man and his tray of food.

"You slept longer than I expected," he told me in that strange, musical tone. "I didn't want to wake you. I want you to feel comfortable and safe in your new home."

"That's very kind of you," I responded, offering a contented sigh as his sincerity engulfed me. He was such a gracious host. Living here would be wonderful. "I'm looking forward to my new life," I told him with complete genuineness.

A look of surprise flashed across his face.

That surprise was enough for me to question myself. I surveyed my wall of protection, still a pile of rubble from the encounter with Tezcatlipoca. These thoughts and emotions were originating with him. They weren't his, exactly. He was creating them somehow in me. I snapped myself out of it and plastered a smile on my face. I needed to distract him while I rebuilt my wall.

The man before me, unaware of my internal discussion, had continued speaking. "I'm so glad to hear you say that. I want you to be happy here."

"Yes, I know I will be," I said. My mind grappled with the pile of stones from my crumbled protective barrier. Lifting a single stone was like lifting a chunk of dense granite. With tremendous effort, I placed one stone and then another. The strength of his overflowing earnestness reduced with each stone I rebuilt in my wall, encouraging my progress.

He indicated the tray of food. "I'll leave this on the dresser for you."

"Why don't you stay and eat with me?" I asked, hoping to sound eager and not like I just didn't want him to lock me up again.

A spike of suspicion slammed into my tenuous wall, almost toppling it again. I quickly created my internal bubble around the suspicion and released it, holding my breath so as not to say anything that would put me in jeopardy.

"You don't have to," I amended my request and then broke eye contact to stare at the carpet. Now a desperate sense of wanting to be liked suffused me. I struggled to keep my breathing steady as I kept his emotions separate from mine while adding more stones. The rubble pile shrank with my effort, and my ability to clear my thoughts improved.

"I'll stay," he stated, then shuffled forward, belying the certainty in his tone. He held the tray out, keeping me at greater than arm's-length distance.

He needn't have worried. I wasn't going to try to swing the tray. Even though, up close, I guessed his height and weight to be around 5'8" and 150 pounds, rather than the 6' from the interaction with the turkey, that still gave him half a foot and half my body weight advantage in a physical confrontation. No, I'd need to use my clairempathy and psychology skills.

"I'm John," he said in a low voice.

"I'm Sarah," I said in a matching tone. "It's nice to meet you."

He offered a shy smile.

"Where are we?" I asked, as if on vacation.

Uncertainty bloomed in his eyes. His bright blue eyes.

"I know you," I blurted out. "You were at the coffeeshop." The repressed memory flooded back in. The intense supernatural energy at the coffeeshop when Kimberly Roberts was leaving. Becoming confused by the crowd of people exiting simultaneously. Locking eyes with a man. A man with bright blue eyes, who I promptly forgot.

He appeared pleased by this outburst. "I waited for you."

"Why didn't I remember you?" I asked, devastated at this level of apparent mind control.

He hesitated in answering and a hardness stole over his features.

I needed a new approach. "I'd like to know more about my new home," I said, deliberately choosing that last word.

He radiated relief. "You're in my home. We are the Kingdom of Tezcatlipoca," he told me with pride.

"That sounds impressive." I frowned. "What is Tez… Tez…" I trailed off, pretending to stumble over the name.

"Tezcatlipoca," he repeated for me, enunciating. "He was an Aztec god." He stopped and watched me expectantly.

Unsure of what he wanted, I loosened a stone in my newly constructed wall to allow my clairempathy to absorb his intentions. "That's impressive," I repeated. "To associate with a god."

"Yes," he enthused, his suspicion almost disappearing.

"How did you choose to name this kingdom after him?" I asked, both out of genuine curiosity, if I was being honest, but also to keep him talking until the cavalry could arrive.

John frowned a moment and a ripple of hurt lapped against my wall. "I had a rough childhood." His face cleared. "Once I became an adult, I wanted to be certain that I was never at anybody else's mercy again." His voice had hardened.

"That sounds difficult," I empathized.

"I found the solution," he said, eyes shining.

"You did?"

"In my research—"

"Research?" I interrupted.

He hesitated, then with a slight shrug, answered. "I was researching the supernatural."

"I'm fascinated by the supernatural," I said, hoping that would keep him talking. He'd shared enough details that my clairempathy was unnecessary to probe what had happened. When John discovered Isabel was a Lechuza and understood what she'd been able to do with that power, he wanted some for himself. It was pure chance that he'd found and connected with the history of Tezcatlipoca.

John eyed me with renewed interest.

I wondered if he sensed my supernatural energy like I sensed his.

"Tezcatlipoca was amazing. The Aztecs called him the trickster god because he would change his name and shapeshift into different animals, depending on his goal. Sometimes he appeared to men as a jaguar, but other times he was a coyote, a vulture, or a—"

"Turkey?" I asked as if I'd just connected the dots from seeing him in his Tezcatlipoca form. I had wondered during my conversation with Isabel if this was a psychological condition or supernatural. His apparent ability to shapeshift had placed my answer firmly in the supernatural camp.

"Yes," he said, his voice giddy. He appeared almost boyish. "He could take on these other forms to entice people to do what he wanted. To be accepted. To be worshipped."

Choosing to side-step the last creepy part of his declaration, I told him, "I understand about being different and wanting to be accepted."

"You do?"

I debated whether to disclose my own supernatural abilities. "I do because I'm a clairempath."

He shook his head.

"That means I can physically and emotionally experience what other people do as if it was happening to me."

His eyes lit up. "I knew I sensed something different about you."

"Not everyone understands the blessing and the curse of that ability." This was a raw truth that I rarely spoke about. I pondered if this was me working a psychological angle, or if his supernatural energy was influencing me. A trickle of sweat rolled down my back at the uncertainty.

"No, they don't." He beamed. "But they will."

"What do you mean?"

He stepped closer as if to confide in me. "I'm building my utopian kingdom to realize the prophecy of Tezcatlipoca's return."

"His return? Aren't you channeling him now?" This was somewhat of a wild guess.

"I am," he said, appearing pleased that I knew. "Once I have enough followers to provide us with energy to thrive on, we will coexist in this body."

Uh-oh. An actual deity existing on our plane again didn't sound like a good idea. That would need to be addressed. But for now, finding the college students was more important. "You said *we* earlier? It isn't going to be just you and me?" I asked innocently.

He placed the food tray on the dresser. "Do you want to know a secret?"

I wordlessly nodded and stepped back, somehow sensing things were going to get weird. Well, weirder.

CHAPTER TWENTY-FOUR

John's bright blue eyes darkened to pitch black, with the sheen of volcanic glass. If he had pupils, they were no longer visible. His frame expanded, and as his clothing tightened on his larger body, the material became hazy. White fuzz sprouted and soon spread across his chest, replacing the fabric. His fingers melded together and as the skin on his lengthening arms lightened, long feathers extended from his newly formed wings. The skin covering his face stretched tight, almost like being pulled back, and soon grew mottled, then solid red, like clay.

Before me stood a man-sized turkey. Tezcatlipoca by way of John Castor, who clearly had some of the same supernatural gifts as his shifter sister.

The turkey's mouth opened. When he spoke, I heard his voice in my ears and reverberating in my mind.

"Come with me," he ordered.

I nodded, understanding that this was the best path forward. Whatever John said was correct. Divine, even.

"Don't try anything stupid," he warned.

"Of course not," I agreed. Why would I risk my chance to live with a god? I'd be silly to mess that up. The stones of my protection wall rained down to the earth in my mind. The feelings ramped up that everything was as it should be. I was thrilled to start this next phase of my life.

The turkey tilted its head, those blank obsidian eyes staring at me. And yet I sensed he was evaluating me. Reaching a decision, he stepped backward toward the door. "Come with me," he repeated and turned to open the door.

With his back turned, the energy within me shifted. Perhaps his hold had lessened. I didn't know, but I embraced the rebellious streak that surfaced. I shook my head to push his powerful, invasive thoughts and emotions from my mind. Freedom! I needed to run.

Closing my eyes, I commanded my mind to cooperate. A headache bloomed and a tingling flash of cold swept over my skin as my barrier stones wobbled on the ground in my mind. Slowly, so slowly, they lifted and floated upward to begin to rebuild my protective wall.

John paused just outside the door. He half-turned, his black eyes pinning me to my spot like a butterfly on a board.

The rebuilding stones crashed to my mind's floor as John's eye contact drained my energy to fight, replaced by a wary but excited energy. I just needed to regain my footing on the path.

Apparently satisfied, he strode forward. I hurried to keep up with his pace. We entered a long, carpeted hallway that I suspected ran the length of the house. The smell of bleach burned my nose—what stains did he need to clean? A row of closed doors lined each side of the hallway. The rust-colored sconces with their Einstein lightbulbs between the doors provided flair. An attempt at an artsy dungeon. This internal joke allowed my self-preservation to fight off his intrusive energy long enough for me to experience a ripple of horror before it crested and his incredible power pushed it down.

John waved a wing at the hallway of doors. "I've only just begun."

"Are there people staying here?" I asked, trying hard to hold on to my humanity and individuality, not allow his divine energy to subsume me. I wondered how many doors had kidnapped women behind them. And then wondered why I didn't feel their energy. Were they okay, or was his energy powerful enough to mask them?

"Three other women so far. Soon, I will recruit more, both men and women, of all ages," he assured me as if seeking my approval. "This is the start of our kingdom. When I have enough, I will merge with Tezcatlipoca reborn, fulfilling the Aztec prophesy." At this pronouncement, his voice echoed in my mind like a blaring alarm.

I gripped the sides of my head in agony and leaned at the waist, gasping to breathe through the pain.

"Sarah?" John asked, his voice softer, unsure.

Tears streamed from my eyes, squeezed shut. I squatted down, rocking back and forth on the soles of my shoes.

Perhaps unsure, given my reaction, the turkey stayed quiet.

The pain receded. My breath evened out. The nauseous roiling of my stomach settled, and I swallowed the acid bile that had surfaced. I swiped a hand across my tear-stained face and stood on shaky feet. My mind was the clearest it had been since I'd met John in his Tezcatlipoca form. I couldn't waste the opportunity.

As I opened my mouth to speak, a loud banging sounded in the house above us. John and I dropped our heads back, both trying to identify the source of the sound. It was an odd visual with a man-sized turkey.

John ordered, "Stay put," at the same time I yelled with all my lung capacity, "We're down here!"

CHAPTER TWENTY-FIVE

John's pupilless eyes drilled into my soul in response to my hollering. "That was a mistake," he said, his guttural voice sounding like multiple voices layered atop one another.

I trembled like a blade of grass in a storm as a strength of emotions I'd never experienced before assaulted my mind. They were so strong, they even overcame my clairempathy and I didn't once believe they were my experiences.

These emotions belonged to an *other*. And that other was the man channeling an Aztec god.

Although my body remained frozen in place, vibrations shook me from head to toe. Tears streamed again from my wide-open eyes. I needed to move, but my legs shuddered with failed attempts to do so. I, instead, focused on a smaller body part, opening and closing my fisted hands dangling limp by my sides. With effort, I unclenched my jaw. The physical distractions enabled my mind to try to identify and isolate the barrage of feelings. At first, all I could do was identify the raw emotions.

Anger.

Sadness.

Fear.

John locked his obsidian eyes onto me, causing me to falter in my progress. "What are you doing?"

I swallowed past the desert inside my throat. "What are you doing?" I countered.

His head jerked like he was trying to avoid an annoying fly.

I wondered at the cause, but he spoke again.

"I will take care of the interlopers."

Closed fists at my side centered me again. "How will you take care of them?" I squeaked out, while also redoubling my effort to identify the emotions. This time, I identified them more completely.

Anger at being denied.

Sadness at being alone.

Fear of failure.

Then a new one. Guilt that this was wrong.

"What are you doing?" John repeated in that guttural, layered voice. Before I could manage an answer, he shook his head again, more forcefully. There was nothing I could see as the cause.

Perhaps I was approaching this the wrong way. Instead of searching for ways to isolate and remove the intrusive emotions, I focused on the guilt. And instead of my modus operandi of wrapping it in a bubble and releasing it, I opened myself up to it. I allowed the guilt to pass over the internal barrier that once again lay in a pile of rubble in my mind. I idly wondered if maybe it was time for a new protective system.

John's guilt filled my mind, flowing into every crevice, every pocket, every opening. I became John's guilt, my clairempathic ability embracing it as my own experience. This wasn't coming from Tezcatlipoca. This was very much from the mind of John Castor. He wanted to fulfill Tezcatlipoca's rebirth prophecy, true, but at least some part of him recognized it as wrong and as an overreaction to his past.

The black eyes of the turkey before me blazed with supernatural fury. "Stop! I feel what you're doing."

"Huh," I eloquently replied. That had never happened before. Other beings didn't have the experiences I did. Then I remembered Tezcatlipoca's additional identity as the God of Smoke and Mirrors. Perhaps our joint experience was reflecting back and forth between us. That certainly could explain the intensity.

"Enough!" John roared, expanding his white wings to their full 10-foot wingspan glory. It was a sight to behold.

The intimidation tactic worked. My brain short-circuited. I stared in wonder at the white quill feathers of his immense wings crowding the hallway.

Dense fog snaked around him, encompassing his body and rising to obscure his face. His eyes glittered in the fog.

My mind hurt from the onslaught. The best choice would be to curl up on the floor to rest until the commotion upstairs had passed. My yawn that had coincided with these drowsy thoughts froze open. It was the fog somehow triggering these responses.

This was a slowed-down version of what had happened on the street in Wichita Falls. I had to fight it off.

I shook my head, much as John had done, attempting to force the unwanted emotions and physical experiences from my mind.

At the same time the turkey took a menacing step toward me, the voices from above rose in volume. I recognized them. John's failure to take a second step toward me suggested he recognized at least one of them, too.

"Yes, John. It's your sister, Isabel," I blurted out. "Let us help you."

CHAPTER TWENTY-SIX

John stood rigid, his red lips thinned tight. The fog receded from around him as the sound of muted, but still audible, voices drifted down from above.

"Let us help you," I repeated, while I hurried to rebuild my protection wall for probably the dozenth time since taking this case.

Footsteps sounded on the stairs at the far end of the hallway. John and I turned to watch jeans-clad legs come into view. A pair of chinos followed them.

Isabel and Dan reached our floor. Both startled when they saw me standing beside the six-foot-tall turkey. Dan remained by the foot of the stairs.

"John!" Isabel cried out and ran to him.

He fluffed his wings aggressively.

She slammed to a halt just outside of arm's reach. "That's how you want to play this?" she asked in a low, dangerous-sounding voice.

He gobbled low in his throat; the first time I'd heard him make a turkey sound. I didn't know if Isabel understood the noise, but she reacted as if she did.

A flash of angry defiance crossed her face. Then her body shifted. Isabel's frame expanded and within seconds she matched his height. Much like her brother, her t-shirt and jeans shimmered before her arms elongated. White feathers sprouted to replace the clothing and skin. Unlike her brother, her face remained the same, an odd juxtaposition of a human face atop a giant white owl.

John ruffled the feathers on his wings again. The high-pitched sound of wind whistling reached my ears. It sounded like it originated outside. I glanced uneasily at the ceiling of the bunker.

Isabel responded to John by attempting to spread her wings. This failed when they reached the walls on either side. I could only imagine how big they were.

"Why are you here?" John asked his sister in that layered, guttural voice. I understood now that this must be the god's influence.

The high-pitched whistling sounded again and Dan's expression told me he heard it too. The two supernatural beings between us were oblivious.

"I'm your sister," she responded, her raspy voice ending in a slight chirp.

"This does not concern you."

"It does," she disagreed. "I love you."

John's wings folded in closer to his body.

Isabel mimicked the movement. "Please, little brother. Let me help you. This isn't necessary."

"I…" his voice trailed off but sounded softer, more human. "I don't know how to stop."

"Tezcatlipoca," she said, startling me and Dan by addressing the god instead of her brother. "You are a creator god. This is beneath you."

"I am a trickster god, too," the turkey bellowed. "I am everything, anywhere I want to be. Nothing is beneath me."

"The world is different now. It isn't like what you're used to."

"The world will bend to my will."

"You'll never have the worshippers you want," she contradicted. "The world has moved on."

"We will entrance them to our will," Tezcatlipoca said, his voice less bombastic, yet somehow scarier, as chills raced up and down my spine.

"Leave my brother."

"No."

The two supernatural beings stared at each other, at a dangerous impasse. Above us, the sound of the wind changed. A loud roar, long and continuous, sounded.

"Tornado?" I mouthed to Dan, who lifted his hands in helplessness.

Without thinking, I imagined a wrecking ball demolishing my wall of protection. I didn't have time to dismantle it stone by stone, nor did I want time to think about the insanity of my next move.

The rush of supernatural energy, physicality, and heightened emotions from the beings in the center of the hallway almost bowled me over. Down the hallway from me, past the supernatural beings, Dan's eyes widened when they met mine. This suggested that my outward appearance might look as ragged as my insides felt.

The onslaught just about incapacitated me. I wove through the swirling mass of emotions, physicality, and streaking colors, filtering Dan's human and Isabel's supernatural energy, until only the pulsing power of Tezcatlipoca remained. Before I could chicken out, I allowed that power to engulf me. Interestingly, as before, a unique twist to my own abilities: I could clearly sense these energies were separate from my own. My clairempathy wasn't activating, for lack of a better word, but my supernatural capacity was.

Although I remained my petite self, my energy felt too big for the contained space. I spread my arms wide. "Listen to me," I roared.

The two birds in the hallway spun to face me.

I glared at Tezcatlipoca. "Enough. You are the creator god," I repeated what Isabel had said. "Do you want to be at the mercy of this human?"

"I am at no human's mercy," he snarled back.

"John is no ordinary human." I tapped into the energy flowing within me. "You can see all the world at all times. You must see that too."

Alarms blaring prevented Tezcatlipoca from responding.

Dan fumbled in his backpack. He pulled both our phones from their depths. "Tornado alert!" He faced the phones toward us. Thank goodness Florida's hurricane season had meant we were signed up for the National Weather Service's emergency alert system that activated nationwide.

Fatigue was stealing over me. I couldn't maintain this level of supernatural energy much longer. And now either north Texas was earning its Tornado Alley reputation or Tezcatlipoca had conjured a freaking tornado. I needed to push him to leave. "There's much more you can do on your own. Leave him to live his life."

"Please, Juan," Isabel joined her voice with mine, using her brother's given name.

The turkey's eyes flashed blue so fast I wasn't sure I saw it. Then, he made a new sound, a soft, rolling gobble. Before I could wonder at the meaning, a gaping emptiness stole over me and I knew Tezcatlipoca pulled his energy. Then, as I watched in awe, John's transformation reversed.

The rough, red skin covering his face became mottled. It loosened, like someone planned to peel it from his skull, then resumed a typical human appearance both in tightness and prior tan color. The tips of his wings split, becoming ten fingers. Those wings shrank down as the feathers melted into the darker, finer hair on his now-human arms. His broadened frame contracted and the white fuzz that had spread across his chest seemed to rotate. Color blossomed in the rotation, like drops of food coloring, and soon his clothing reappeared.

I idly wondered how his clothes survived these transformations and decided this was a tiny detail to just accept.

The obsidian eyes were the last to revert. Black lightened. Pupils became defined. Bright blue replaced the sheen of volcanic glass.

Beads of sweat on John's forehead were the only physical sign that his body had just undergone an extraordinary transformation.

CHAPTER TWENTY-SEVEN

"John!" Isabel cried out, running to engulf her baby brother in a tight hug. Wait, when did she transform back into a human? I was so wrapped up in John's transformation that I must have missed it.

Dan ran from the foot of the stairs past them. "Doc," he said as he reached where I stood swaying with utter satisfied exhaustion. He wrapped his arms around me, the sour scent of anxious body odor wafting from him. "Never do that again," he whispered, though we both knew that directive fell on deaf ears. I'd do whatever the case needed.

"Thank you for rescuing us," I said to them both after they'd released us from their hugs. Our foursome stood awkwardly.

Isabel spoke first. "How did—" She waved one arm up and down to indicate his figure.

He understood the question. "That's a long story. The abbreviated version is simple. I freaked out when I learned you were a Lechuza."

"How did you find out?"

He offered a lop-sided grin. "I'm no genius, but even I caught on that every single time I told you about someone bothering me, they stopped shortly after and a rumor of a Lechuza sighting popped up."

Her cheeks reddened. "Okay. Yeah. I guess that would have been obvious if you knew what to look for. Why did you freak out?" she added, almost as an afterthought.

He snorted. "I discovered my sister was a supernatural being when I was 18 years old?"

"Fair enough," she said with a laugh.

"I fled El Paso and bounced around for a few years." His eyes misted and I knew those must have been challenging times. "It occurred to me that since you had a supernatural gift, maybe I did, too. I spent a lot of time in libraries, using the free internet to read about the history of the supernatural in different cultures, trying to learn everything I could." His eyes blazed in a way that made me uneasy. "That was when I stumbled across Tezcatlipoca."

"That's where you stopped?" Isabel asked.

He nodded. "Something about him called to me in a way that nothing else I read had."

"There's a difference between having a theoretical understanding of this and doing what you did," I interrupted.

"An excellent point," he conceded. "I don't have a good explanation, to be honest." He shrugged. "I meditated on it, called for Tezcatlipoca's guidance, and just *knew* that one day he would answer. And then one day, I heard a voice in my head."

"That must have been terrifying," Isabel said.

"It was! I wondered if I was having a psychotic break."

"That could have been true," I said, glad it wasn't a psychotic break, but not sure how much better it had been channeling an Aztec god.

"But," he continued, "I answered the voice. Our plan developed over time, with him providing guidance." He spread his arms wide. "And here we are."

"Now what?" Isabel directed that question more to me than to her brother.

"The first order of business is releasing the kidnapped women and bringing them for medical evaluation," I stated.

John shook his head. "With Tezcatlipoca gone from my mind, all I can think of is how terrifying this must have been for them." He appeared stricken. "Don't worry. I'll turn myself in to the police."

"No!"

All eyes swung to Isabel.

"Please," she begged me. "Let me help him."

"I don't think—" I started.

"This is my fault," she interrupted. "Or at least, it began with me," she hastened to add when I lifted my hand to object.

I considered what she was saying. What would happen to John if he went into the system? Either prison or a mental hospital. That wasn't what someone with strong supernatural abilities needed. He needed someone to guide him and keep him on the right path.

"Sarah?" Isabel asked into my continued silence.

"I think that's the best option," I answered her.

"You do?" John asked with a hopeful inflection.

Dan stayed silent, probably having gone through the same internal monologue that I had.

"I do," I answered John before facing Isabel and taking her hands in mine. I removed a stone from my internal barrier to get a flavor of her emotions when I made my next statement. "John will need your guidance. Your protection. Most importantly, your love."

Her eyes shined with unshed tears. "I promise to stay with him through everything," she assured me. The truth of her statement flowed as a heady mix of relief, love, and determination in my mind.

"I believe you," I told her.

"I'll help him back on the path. He won't harm anyone again." She released my hands and reached one out to her brother. "We'll both get the help we need to deal with our pasts."

The word *trauma* remained unspoken, but since that was the catalyst for them unlocking their latent supernatural abilities, I agreed it was important to address.

"How will you handle the police?" John asked with trepidation.

"The two of you leave now," I instructed. "Dan and I will bring the women upstairs. We'll call the detective and tell him we received a tip of their location…" Here I looked to Dan to confirm our location.

"That the women were in an underground bunker outside of Wichita Falls," he completed my sentence.

"Will that work?" Isabel asked.

"Maybe, maybe not," I admitted. "But it will buy you and John—"

"It's Juan," her brother corrected me, almost shyly.

"It will buy you and Juan time to cover your tracks and establish a new life elsewhere." I shifted my gaze between them. "A new life free of drama."

"We promise," Isabel said and Juan echoed.

"You should probably get going," I said.

Isabel threw her arms around me in a brief hug. "Thank you for everything."

Juan withdrew a key from his pocket. "I'm so sorry for everything. I don't understand how it all went sideways."

"Make sure nothing like this ever happens again," I told him as I accepted the key.

"None of them were hurt." Sorrow and guilt streamed from him to me.

"Physically," I reminded him.

He inclined his head. "Yes."

"However, that's one reason I'm allowing this plan," I responded. "Now go."

Isabel grabbed her brother's hand. They raced toward the stairs and their new lives together.

CHAPTER TWENTY-EIGHT

A frenzied week followed the day's events at the Kingdom of Tezcatlipoca. Detective Brad Snyder's consternation increased the more I offered the same polite, if vague, answers to his repeated questions. I understood. As a law enforcement officer, his mandate was to see justice done; and, in his mind, that meant whoever kidnapped the women needed to be behind bars. Yet, I sensed he understood where Dan and I were coming from as well, and since the women were safely back with their loved ones, he finally gave us the green light to leave Wichita Falls.

Now we sat in a restaurant at Dallas's Love Field Airport, enjoying the spicy scent of Mexican food while savoring preflight cocktails to celebrate the case's successful conclusion.

Dan lifted his classic margarita to toast. I joined him with my pomegranate margarita, with sugar on the rim instead of salt, of course.

"To a reasonably happy ending," he toasted.

"To a reasonably happy ending," I echoed.

We sipped our drinks and a sense of melancholy hit me. I prodded it, not surprised to identify it wasn't my emotion.

"What's the matter?" I asked.

He laughed. "That's not fair."

"I'd say it's an occupational hazard, but...." I shrugged.

"I'm sorry."

"For what?" I asked, baffled.

"For taking so long to get there." He sipped his drink. "It took longer to track you than we'd expected."

"You got there when it mattered," I said, though my mind flashed back to my terror at the discovery of the locked door trapping me with a supernatural being channeling an Aztec god.

"Still." He shook his head. "Your tracker flickered in and out. We had a hard time fixing on the signal."

"It was probably the bunker," I told him.

"We guessed that when we realized you were underground."

"I freaked out a little," I admitted, "when I had the thought that the tracker might not work."

"What if it never steadied?" he asked in a tight voice.

"It did," I reminded him, using my free hand to give his a comforting squeeze.

"Do you think Juan was Tezcatlipoca?" Dan asked.

I accepted his abrupt topic change with relief. "Honestly? It's hard to say. There's no question Juan shifted into Tezcatlipoca's trickster form."

"Couldn't that just be like Isabel's shifting into Lechuza?" he asked. "After all, that's what her being a Lechuza boils down to, since she doesn't take babies or kill people."

"That's a reasonable alternative hypothesis. But the otherness I experienced tells me Juan really channeled Tezcatlipoca." I swigged my margarita to quench the sudden desert in my throat at the memory of the Aztec god's emotions in my mind.

"Do you think they'll stay ahead of the law?" he asked.

"I hope so."

"It was helpful that none of the women were able to physically describe their kidnapper."

"Indeed it was." I cupped my margarita glass with both hands, enjoying the chilled condensation. "Isabel didn't do anything except help Juan get away, so the worst charge she could get would be aiding and abetting. Juan Garcia has no record since high school, and John Castor simply appeared then disappeared."

"It was also helpful that he'd just been squatting on that property," Dan pointed out.

"Agreed. Can you imagine the property owner's shock when he learned an entire home was built in the middle of his land without his knowledge?" I snort-laughed at my imagined scene of the out-of-town property owner driving up to the ranch home.

"Thank goodness we rescued the college students and they're receiving therapy through the university," Dan said. "And that Isabel will make sure Juan receives the help he needs."

"She's his family. She can protect him. And protect others from him."

"Good thing we got the retainer upfront. It's a shame we didn't get the balance," Dan joked. "Although doing pro bono work is good for the soul."

"Oh, I didn't tell you?" I responded.

He quirked an eyebrow. "Tell me what?"

"When I was checking out of the hotel and you were getting the car, the front desk clerk handed me an envelope that had been left for me."

Dan belly laughed. "Someone left you an envelope filled with money?"

"Someone did." I sipped at my margarita, enjoying the merriment.

"I guess someone planned ahead."

"Someone had a lot of foresight," I agreed.

Dan lifted his glass again to toast, and I matched with mine.

"To a happy ending," he amended his toast from before.

"To a happy ending," I said. "You might have to edit some of this one before putting it on your *A Doctor Danger Mystery* blog."

"No doubt," he agreed. He lifted his drink.

"Another toast?" I teased.

"To our next supernatural adventure," he said.

"To our next supernatural adventure," I echoed, eager to discover what that might entail. Our lives were certainly never boring.

Writing this book was an absolute joy. If you've read my other books featuring Doctor Sarah Danger, then you know I visit those locations as a big part of my research. *Trickster in Texas* went much deeper than that. I lived all over Texas for pushing twenty years, including over three years in Wichita Falls while stationed at Sheppard Air Force Base during my tour of duty with the United States Public Health Service. Yep, I was a Lieutenant Commander. It's hard to believe sometimes, to be honest. That part of my life in uniform was a long time ago.

However. I loved living in Wichita Falls. There's a thriving theater arts scene, and I performed in a variety of fabulous musicals while living there, including *Cinderella*, *Hairspray*, *Seven Brides for Seven Brothers*, and *Camelot*. I also made strong friendships, including with a woman I consider my "twin sister" and with whom I am still in constant contact.

It had been over a decade since I lived in Wichita Falls, and so I stayed with my friend before writing this book. I had a blast seeing how much the town had changed and how much had remained the same. I also must thank her for doing last-minute runs around town, double-checking my memories, though of course, all mistakes are my own.

Note that, as with all of my books that take place in real locales, this book is a mix of fact and fiction. All the places with names are real places in Texas except for the micronation. I created Juan's kingdom based on a ton of research into existing and former micronations. None of the characters are based on real people, even if I did use jumbled versions of some of their names for fun.

I truly hope you enjoyed Doctor Danger's latest adventure and spending time in Wichita Falls, a place I once called home.

If you enjoy flirty romance with your paranormal mysteries, check out the completed *Paranormal Talent Agency* series today!

PARANORMAL TALENT AGENCY

Lights, Camera, Action (PTA, #1)

Welcome to the Paranormal Talent Agency!

When empath Catherine Rodham moves across the country to launch the west coast arm of the Peterson Talent Agency in Las Vegas, her plan goes awry when an actress on a film she helped cast turns up murdered, leaving law enforcement stumped.

Alex Moore, a Sin City actor with a secret, wants agency representation from Catherine – and maybe something more. But everything changes after he finds himself the target of a murder investigation.

When the two team together to solve the serial murders, Alex introduces Catherine to a paranormal underworld she never knew existed. Can Catherine prove Alex's innocence before losing her heart…or her life?

PARANORMAL TALENT AGENCY

Reset to One (PTA, #2)

The Paranormal Talent Agency Saga Continues

All vampire Evie Jones desires is to enjoy her fun immortal life as an actress. Until she meets fellow actor Ryan Walter, who intrigues her with his insistence that his best friend has been framed for murder.

The appearance of her movie producer ex-husband in Sin City complicates Evie's offer to team with Ryan to find the real killer. She wants nothing to do with her ex, but he may hold the key to more than one murder.

Amid their growing attraction, and with the help of her Paranormal Talent Agency friends, can Evie and Ryan solve the murders…and find their happily ever after?

PARANORMAL TALENT AGENCY

That's a Wrap (PTA, #3)

Mid-Season Finale of the Paranormal Talent Agency

Mia Fynn, a nixie who has lived among humans for over 200 years, loves her life as a producer in Sin City. When the lead actor in her upcoming movie is murdered during a live social media video, Mia finds herself thrust into the role of detective.

Jacob Dawson, an actual Las Vegas Metro Police Department detective, would rather not have Mia's assistance. But even he can't deny the literal sparks that fly whenever they touch.

With the help of her Paranormal Talent Agency friends and one nosy television reporter, Mia scrambles to catch a killer... and reel in her own true love.

PARANORMAL TALENT AGENCY

An Unexpected Sequel (PTA, #4)

Mid-Season Premiere of the Paranormal Talent Agency

Five years ago, a desperate witch made a pact with a demon. Now Robin Landon, the owner of Landon Talent Agency, splits her time between managing the actors she represents and laboring as a demon's minion.

When Robin refuses the demon's order to kill Jackson McKee, a witch with a day job as a camera operator, she must balance her growing feelings for the intended target and evading the vengeful demon's wrath.

Out of options, Robin turns to her former nemeses with the Paranormal Talent Agency. Will their daring plan save Jackson from the demon, or will Robin lose both her chance at love and her life?

PARANORMAL TALENT AGENCY

Jumping the Shark (PTA, #5)

The Penultimate Episode of the Paranormal Talent Agency

Demon Barbara Knollman enjoys her reign as the head of Las Vegas and barely tolerates the necessity of running for office. But when her precognitive abilities save her from an attack on the candidates, she becomes both target and suspect.

Uncertain of her next steps, Barbara agrees to help angel Liam Collins stop a supernatural being hellbent on taking control of the paranormal world by whatever means necessary. And wonders if she's heading down a path of no return.

Accused of murder and with her demonic powers on the fritz, Barbara allows Liam to convince her to team with the Paranormal Talent Agency. Can Barbara clear her name, stop a killer… and open her dark heart to true love?

PARANORMAL TALENT AGENCY

The Season Finale (PTA, #6)

The Exciting Conclusion of the Paranormal Talent Agency

Television reporter Elizabeth "Liz" Addison is investigating the supernatural story of a lifetime. Except she doesn't know what it is, just who it is – Catherine Rodham, owner of the Paranormal Talent Agency.

Liz knows she's on the right track when a time-traveling ghost warns her that she'll die if she continues the investigation. She ignores the threats until her romantic interest in Antonio "Tony" DiMaio, the were-panther owner of *Soprannaturale,* puts him directly in the supernatural line of fire.

To save Tony and uncover the truth about Catherine, Liz and the Paranormal Talent Agency join together for one last wild adventure in the paranormal world of Las Vegas!

THANK YOU

Thank you so much for supporting my work and reading this novel.

If you liked the book, please consider leaving a review online.

Just a few lines would be great. Reviews are not only the highest compliment you can pay to an author, they also help other readers discover and make more informed choices about purchasing books in a crowded online space. Thank you so much in advance.

If you didn't like the book or have concerns,
please email me directly at
heather@heathersilvio.com

ABOUT THE AUTHOR

Heather Silvio loves to tell stories, especially fun, fast-paced, paranormal mysteries & flirty romance. She is also an actress and licensed psychologist with a few nonfiction titles for variety. When she isn't working, she channels her inner flapper as a 1920s jazz and blues singer.

Visit https://www.heathersilvio.com for more information and to sign up for her Theatrical Thursdays Newsletter.

9 781951 192419